ILLEGALLY INNOCENT

ILLEGALLY INNOCENT

ANGELA BACON

MILL CITY PRESS | MINNEAPOLIS

Mill City Press, Inc.
212 3rd Avenue North, Suite 290
Minneapolis, MN 55401
612.455.2294
www.millcitypublishing.com

ISBN-13: 978-1-938223-41-9
LCCN: 2012940106

Author photo used by permission from Jamie Brokus

References to Dr. Hulda Clark's book *The Cure for HIV and AIDS* used by permission
from Geoffrey Clark

Book Design by Kristeen Ott

Printed in the United States of America

ACKNOWLEDGMENTS

Thank You, God, for Your blessing of parents, grandparents, family members, friends, teachers, and professors who have all been supportive of my dream to become a published writer. Over the years, they have read my stories and offered encouraging words and helpful advice. When I was a kid, my parents spent thousands of hours driving me to bookstores and libraries, and they regularly visited my homemade library on the basement couch, stocked with handwritten stories about my pets. They also patiently and lovingly endured the "Do not disturb… Writing in progress…Please pass notes under the door" signs on my bedroom door while I wrote mysteries about crime-solving children and all thirty stories of "The Land of Falling Art Supplies" series.

Thanks to all of my friends and family who read various drafts of *Illegally Innocent*, and thank you to those who offered feedback on a section or all of it (in alphabetical order): Amanda, Julie, Koty, Lynn, and Mike.

Thank you to Geoffrey Clark for giving me permission to include mention of Dr. Hulda Clark and her discoveries about disease.

Finally, thank you to those of you who have picked up this book and have dared to try a new author! I would love to hear from you at www.angelabaconbooks.com.

CHAPTER ONE

I awoke to Jake muttering under his breath and my stomach churning angrily. Uncertain as to what was going on, I glanced at Jake and, noticing that he was spending an awful lot of time looking in the rearview mirror, I followed his example and looked in my side mirror.

Police lights flashed one hundred feet behind us in the fog.

All of the fear that we'd experienced before returned at a new level. Everything was much more serious now that we actually had the products in our possession. It was easy to lie about our plans to the cop before, when we didn't have any evidence to suggest otherwise…but now…

"What *now*? What do I do?" Jake whispered. "What do I *say*, Grace?" He shakily swerved over to the gravel, palming a small bottle of Intenzyme Forte resting in the ashtray and thrusting it under his seat before coming to a complete stop.

I struggled to remember why it had seemed like such a great idea to continue with my career once it became illegal.

#
Four years earlier

"I can't wait to get out of here." Fellow English-class warrior Rhonda VanDeMort flagged a page in an Edith Wharton biography with a bright pink Post-it and set her head down on the table, the book flipping shut with a soft clunk.

Fumes from the musty, yellowed piece of literature drifted my way. I accidentally dragged in a deep breath of it and sneezed.

"Jackson's going to kill me," Rhonda whined. "She gave me an extension last semester for my final paper in Brit. lit., and I'm scared to ask for another one, but I'm going to fail this paper if I have to turn it in tomorrow by noon. I've slept about four hours the past two days, and I still only have three pages typed."

I clicked on print preview and sighed at my four pages of writing that more closely resembled notes rather than the coherent, senior-level paper that it needed to be. "I'm already planning to turn it in a day late. She'll only take it down half a letter grade for that." Or maybe I would just turn it in on time as it was. This was the last paper of my undergrad career, and I just didn't care. I hadn't cared much at all during the past eight weeks when I realized that there wasn't anything that I wanted to do with my English degree. I used to think I wanted to be a journalist, but writing for the campus newspaper for two semesters had shown me that was not the path I wanted to take.

Rhonda, on the other hand, was already accepted at a grad school for the upcoming fall semester. Her grades were slightly more important to her than mine were to me. "I would do that, too, but I still need to spend some time studying for the Shakespeare final. One extra day for this paper isn't going to be enough."

It was good that I'd taken Shakespeare last semester. I would probably just quit school altogether if I still had another exam for which to study, especially one as complex as Shakespeare.

I looked up at a familiar face peering through the narrow window in the door. Rhonda and I were sitting in a group study room in the library, and it was customary for other students to peek in to see if the room was empty. Small grid lines traced across the glass, forming diamond-shaped spaces to smudge—some bored student had already pressed his or her lips to the surface in three spots, and someone else had come up with the idea of placing one fingerprint inside each diamond but must have been interrupted by an angry librarian when just halfway completed with the task. I was distracted every single time someone walked by, whether he or she actually looked in the window or not. I was also distracted by the occasional bursts of loud laughter from the group study room next door and by the fly whizzing past my ear every few minutes. I had studied the various scratches in the door several times, running through name possibilities for some initials carved into a small heart near one of the hinges. All in all, I was accomplishing virtually nothing, and I had been sitting in this scuffed-up desk chair for an hour and a half.

I motioned for the person at the door to come in. Candace McCormick lived just down the hall from me; we'd been friends since sophomore year, when she nearly beat down my door in the middle of the night to tell me that one of her gold mollies was giving birth, and she wondered if I wanted to watch the event. Procrastinator that I am, I was not in bed at 2 a.m. when she knocked, and watching a fish give birth sounded much more interesting than studying for a biology mid-term. We kept our eyes on that molly until 4:30, whispering to each other in an effort not to wake up her roommate. When I asked Candace why she'd picked my door, she shrugged and replied, "You're the only one in our hall who I always see up at this time of night. I figured that tonight would be like all the other nights and that you'd still be up."

It was true. I frequently passed Candace at 1 or 2 in the morning, on my way to brush my teeth or throw some laundry in a dryer. She tended to study just outside her room door. Her roommate could not handle any light while sleeping, and so if Candace wanted to accomplish anything after her roommate went to bed at the typical 11:30 time, she had to go somewhere other than the room. Candace and I usually just smiled at each other in passing, and I had never tried talking to her before that night. We bonded over procrastination, chocolate mint Pop-Tarts, and the strangeness of fish birth.

Candace swung open the group study room door and plopped down in the squeaky seat across from me. Her dark, shoulder-length hair was French-braided back, short layers poking out here and there, while side-swept bangs dangled into her blue eyes.

Her arms were wonderfully free of books and I couldn't help but be envious. "Are you finished with exams?" I asked.

She nodded, a satisfied smile beaming on her face. "Yes, I am. I just turned in the last of my library books and paid off my late fines. Now all I have to do is finish packing and wait for commencement."

"What's your major again?" Rhonda asked Candace. The two of them only knew each other through me.

"Communication Arts."

"What do you want to do with that?" Rhonda twirled a gel pen between her fingers like a baton, back and forth, pinkie to index.

"Nothing, actually. I picked it freshman year because it sounded like a fun major, and I thought about switching a few different times, but nothing ever sounded any better. I'm going to start classes next month to become a bioenergetic practitioner," Candace stated proudly, straightening up in her chair.

"What is that?" Rhonda asked, her nose crinkling at the strange phrase.

Candace had explained this job to me before, but each time I heard her explain it to someone else I understood the concept a little better. It was interesting but slightly unbelievable at the same time. "I'll be like a doctor, except I'll use vitamins and natural remedies to help my patients instead of the kind of medicine everyone thinks of as 'normal.'" She made quote marks in the air. "Instead of having X-rays taken or blood samples drawn or other *typical* medical tests, the patient puts his or her right hand on a hand cradle, which is attached to a computer. The hand cradle is like a large computer mouse, but it has a spot for each of the fingers and the thumb. The best thing to compare it all to is a lie detector test, in which the lie detector picks up on the energy in your body to decide whether you're telling the truth or not. In bioenergetic testing, the computer program figures out the weak areas in your body by sending electrical signals to the body through the hand cradle. It's like it's asking the body questions about its health, and then the energy in your body answers those questions."

I looked at Rhonda out of the corner of my eye and could tell that she was trying hard to pay attention but that she really hadn't expected to get such an in-depth response to her polite question.

"The program sorts through the information your body gives it and lists the areas that are of the most concern to your body at that moment," Candace continued. "For example, maybe you have a bacterial infection in your throat—if that was one of the worst problems in your body at that moment, your throat would be listed among the top problems. The practitioner then uses the program and his or her knowledge of nutritional supplements to suggest the best vitamins and herbal remedies that the patient could take to clear out the illness.

"The more you cleanse out the different viruses, bacteria, parasites, and other stuff, you move down through the layers in the body. You come up with new stuff to get rid of that was hidden before because it wasn't one of the things that your body felt it needed to fight off right away—your body had other, more important problems. So, the more frequently you're tested, the more often you can change your homeopathy or herbs or whatever to match what's wrong in your body, and you can get healthier quicker. I won't be a *real* doctor, so I can't actually *diagnose*, but I can highly recommend."

"There's a big market for that sort of thing?" Rhonda asked skeptically, whirling pen momentarily suspended between middle and ring fingers.

"You'd be surprised," Candace answered. "I just found out about it a couple of years ago, and the bioenergetic practitioner I've been going to is always booked at least five weeks in advance. I think it's way more interesting than anything in Comm. Arts. So that's what I'm going to do." She shrugged.

I wondered how it would feel to be so sure of myself. I would give anything to have something concrete to tell people about my future plans—as it stood, I wasn't about to get married like tons of my friends were, I had no idea what I was going to do for a job other than a standing offer from Applebee's to return to my waitressing job from the previous summer, and I hadn't applied to grad school. I didn't even have an apartment lined up or own a car.

"Hmmm," Rhonda said. She started twirling the pen again and became a little too interested in her paper.

I was proud of Candace for being willing to do something so strange. I was afraid to tell my parents that I didn't want to be a journalist, now that I'd put so much time and money into becoming one. I couldn't imagine what they'd say if I randomly told them that I wanted to do something crazy that they'd never heard of, like Candace's bioenergetic practitioner job.

"Anyway, I stopped by to see if you wanted to go to dinner with me, Grace," Candace invited, seemingly oblivious to Rhonda's lack of enthusiasm over her career plan. "You're welcome to come too, if you want, Rhonda."

"Dinner sounds great," I exclaimed, packing up my laptop and the stack of books beside it. The paper could wait an hour. "Wanna come, Rhonda?"

"I really need to get some work done," she answered. "I might stop by in a little bit. I should try to get out another page or so first."

"Okay." I stood, twenty-pound book bag slung over my shoulder, and eagerly followed Candace out of the library. Exhausted students surrounded the collection of desktop computers on the main floor, battered textbooks and reference materials splayed out across the tables and carpet. A couple of students prowled around the area like hungry cougars, silently pressuring the others to desert their computers so that they could have a chance to work on their own papers. One girl, in full exam-week mode with a hoodie, sweatpants, messy bun, thick glasses, and not a trace of makeup, shot a dirty look at the guy hovering close to her shoulder, who was clearly planning to slide into her swivel chair as soon as she vacated it.

The late afternoon air was stifling, considering that it was only the first week of May in Indiana. Perspiration swelled on my upper lip just during the walk from the library to the cafeteria, and I wished that I had changed into a short-sleeved shirt when I'd been in my dorm room a few hours earlier. Candace and I passed a bench on our walk; a freshman couple occupied it, firmly entwined in each other's arms. The girlfriend's head rested on her boyfriend's shoulder while he stroked her long hair, a daydreamy expression on both of their faces. I gagged quietly, and Candace laughed, nodding in agreement. Although we attended a campus of 12,000 students, I somehow managed to come across this particular couple at least twice a week, either sitting on one of the outdoor benches or holding hands in the cafeteria and staring into each others' eyes while eating their meals.

The cafeteria was half-full with students who had decided that it was a better option to spend their time studying in close proximity to food as opposed to trying to find an open cubicle or empty room in the library. Wherever I looked, students with their open textbooks, pages of notes, and flashcards sipped at cappuccinos and Mountain Dew, massaging out headaches with ink-stained fingertips and rubbing at weary, bloodshot eyes with their palms. I tripped over a backpack on my way to survey the dinner choices, and the plastic cup of water in my hand sloshed onto the floor and the tennis shoe of a guy passing me. He swore at me, shaking his head, and I gritted my teeth, trying not to be angry with him. Everyone was stressed right now, and I had probably done several things already that week which were unnecessarily spiteful toward other people.

I ate my usual taco salad with ice cream for dessert, while Candace dutifully consumed an apple and a plate full of dry salad with grilled chicken strips. I shook my head. "Your self-discipline is amazing," I told her. Occasionally I ate the same way, but mostly I was waiting to change my eating habits post-college. I had gained twelve pounds over my four years of college; another three days of eating junk food was not going to drastically affect anything.

"I'm trying to eat extra healthy because I'm planning to do a cleanse next week," she explained. "Hopefully the better I take care of myself now, the less sick I'll be while I detox."

I nodded as if I understood. I had no idea what she was talking about. A cleanse? Getting sick from it? Didn't sound like anything I wanted to talk about while eating taco salad, which already looked kind of pre-digested, what with all the salsa and nacho cheese and suspicious-looking ground beef mixed together over stringy iceberg lettuce and crumpled-up chips. My glob of sour cream rolled down the messy hill and onto the edge of my plate. Half of it fell onto the table, but I just left it, figuring that I would probably spill something else and may as well clean it all up at once when I was finished with my supper.

"So what should we do when you come visit me in a few weeks?" Candace asked brightly.

One of the things getting me through exam week was the exciting idea that Candace and I would get to hang out together soon, without all the worry and stress of homework. We lived three hours apart, and I'd never been to her house before. With summer open before us, we hadn't even planned how long I would stay with her, just that I was coming over. At this point I wasn't sure how I was going to have the money to do that, but I would worry about that later. My job at Applebee's was looking better and better every minute.

CHAPTER TWO

Later that night, while I was eking out a sixth page of my paper, I decided to take a break and visit Candace. The resident director had made us pull all of our hall decorations down at the beginning of exam week, exposing the pockmarks and leftover shreds of poster putty and tape from years past. It was fairly dark in the hall this time of night, but I still knew where the stain was and stepped carefully over it. Earlier in the year, there had been a "mouse incident," in which a girl named Andrea was cleaning her room and a furry little creature ran out from her room into the hall. Because Andrea couldn't think of anything else to do, she threw one of her roommate's shoes at the mouse, somehow managing to actually hit it and smashing the rodent into the carpet. The cleaning ladies had brought in a Rug Doctor the next day to try to get the nasty mouse-gut stain out of the carpet, but to this day there was still a faint spot that they had never been able to fully remove. We had a girl in our hall who considered that stain to be a good luck charm and purposely walked on it whenever she had to take an exam; I avoided the stain at all costs.

The hall smelled of just-microwaved Ramen noodles and hot chocolate mixed with Lysol and laundry detergent. Kanye West drifted out from the closed bathroom door, accompanied by the echo of poorly-performed shower rapping. I found Candace in her usual spot, exiled there by her sleeping roommate. Since Candace didn't have any homework left to do, she was apparently reading for fun, although when I glanced at the titles of the books surrounding her, I had a difficult time understanding why this was pleasure reading. She grinned when I asked her why she was reading a book about parasites and their effect on the colon.

"It's really interesting, Grace. I need to learn all about this stuff if I'm going to start my training next month. Here, read this one. I was looking through it earlier today." Candace handed over a thick book about alternative treatments for diabetes. I settled in against the wall next to her and opened it up.

I lost three hours' worth of work on my paper that night to her stupid book, and I was shocked when I realized it was 3:30. I reluctantly set the book aside and returned to my room, growling to myself over the disgraceful state of my last paper and how much I didn't want to work on it.

# # #

I borrowed one of my parents' cars to drive to Candace's house several weeks later. Halfway there, the air conditioning broke, and a few minutes after that, I realized that I was lost. I tried to call Candace but could only reach her voicemail, so I ended up stopping at four different businesses before someone could give me directions that made sense. I arrived at Candace's front door sweaty and overheated with a resolve to get the car fixed before making the trek home.

Candace lived with her parents in a three-story house surrounded by twenty-five acres of land, the majority of which was thickly-wooded with pines. A pole barn, its siding tan to match the house, rested thirty yards away. The driveway forked off to lead up to the door of the barn. A red maple guarded each side of the house, the two leafy shadows overlapping.

I was confused at the worried look on Candace's face when she opened the door. After a brief hug, she apologized profusely. "Grace, I can't believe it's worked out this way, but I have to start my training tomorrow. I have class from ten to two, four days a week. I thought the start of the new semester was still a couple of weeks away, but I guess I looked at the schedule wrong. I just found out a couple of hours ago."

"Oh." Perhaps my response should have been disappointment and a little bit of anger that I had driven all this way for nothing. However, all I could think about was whether I might be able to attend class with her.

"So I don't know how much hanging out we're going to be able to do since I'll have class and homework," Candace continued, "but you're welcome to stay as long as you like. I am so sorry about this."

I had spent the past month thinking a lot about what I wanted to do for my career now that college was over. I had temporarily taken the waitressing job at Applebee's, but the occupational possibility that consumed my thoughts the most was that of bioenergetic practitioner. I had no idea if I would actually like it, but I hadn't been this excited about something in a long time, and I was seriously considering giving it a try. "May I come to class with you?"

She looked startled. "I guess they probably wouldn't mind if you came for one day or something. Really? You want to do that?"

"I do." I didn't realize it at the time, but that typical marriage phrase ended up being my long-term commitment to the career of bioenergetic practitioner. I went to class with Candace the first day, loved every minute of it, and ended up taking out yet another loan to pay for more education. For some reason, science and medicine fascinated me in a way those subjects never before had. I felt like I had found what I was born to do, not just a job to pass the time and pay my bills. I was going to help people get well, and I was excited about it. I spent the whole summer at Candace's house, keeping my phone calls to my parents concise and far-between so as to hear the least resistance from them toward my newest aspiration.

One day halfway through the summer, I was hurriedly blow-drying my hair while brushing my teeth, trying to regain the time I had lost by accidentally sleeping in. I wrinkled my sun-burnt nose at the reflection in the mirror, blue toothbrush clenched between teeth that should have had braces years ago. It was already 9:40, and I had a fifteen-minute drive to class. Candace had left earlier in order to run a couple of errands, and her parents both had to be at their jobs by 7 a.m., so I never saw them in the mornings. In my rush, I became a little too preoc-cupied with getting myself ready in as short a time as possible and slammed the hairdryer into my head. I had flicked the warm appliance off and was rubbing my skull when the doorbell rang.

Startled, I pondered whether or not to answer the door. After a few short days of staying at the McCormicks', I had realized that it was just best for me not to look outside unless absolutely necessary. All of the shadows and trees shifting in the wind creeped me out.

The doorbell rang again, followed by some knocking. I walked quickly into the guest bedroom that the McCormicks had given me and looked out one of the windows, trying to see who could be standing at the door one floor below. I could tell it was a man, but he definitely did not look familiar. Of course, I could only see the top of his head and what he was wearing, so he could have been one of my relatives, and I wouldn't have known the difference. His grungy appearance concerned me, though. Even from above I could easily pick out splotches of mud on his T-shirt and battered tennis shoes that looked as though they had been through a war. There was no car in the driveway, which had to mean that he had walked up (extra creepy), and his body language translated into anger and frustration.

I shuddered and backed away from the window, returning to the bathroom to put on my makeup. I would just ignore him, and he would go away eventually, right? I was already going to be late to class without this interruption, anyway. What were a few more minutes?

I was smearing foundation across my forehead when I heard the front door unlock and swing open; I set down the small plastic tube and grabbed my cell phone from off the counter. I ducked quickly into the guest bedroom again and noted with rising panic that the man who had been standing at the front door was no longer there. There still weren't any vehicles in the driveway, which unfortunately meant that neither Candace nor one of her parents had returned to the house. The person who I could now hear walking around in the kitchen had to be the strange man.

I grabbed a large pair of scissors from Candace's mom's sewing room, thinking that I might be able to use them as a weapon. I kept my cell phone in the other hand and forced myself to go downstairs.

I could hear the refrigerator door open and some cupboards slam shut. Had the bum broken into the house just to get something to eat? I slunk down the carpeted stairs and tripped over the man's shoes, which were lying near the front door. My scissors clattered to the wooden floor, and suddenly all was silent in the kitchen.

I held my breath and bent down to pick up my weapon.

The footsteps that came toward me were accompanied by the crackling of a bag of chips. I raised my arm up by my head and positioned the scissors in my hand so as to stab with the most force possible if necessary.

The man, who looked to be about my age, jumped when he rounded the corner and saw my hand up by my face, scissors ready to be thrust into him with a burst of adrenaline at a moment's notice. He gasped, and I thought I saw a tiny bit of fear in his eyes.

That's right. You should be afraid, Dude.

Now that I was up close and took a better look, the thought occurred to me that his cocoa-colored hair was too perfectly gelled and the sunglasses perched on top of his head appeared too expensive for him to be a hobo, but just because someone had money, that didn't make him any less of a threat. I didn't back off but did shiver nervously.

He reached into the bag again and carefully set a tortilla chip in his mouth, staring at me the whole time. "Did you just break in?" he asked cautiously. "Why are you in this house?"

"What are *you* doing in this house?" I flung back at his six-foot-tall self, hostility lacing my tone. Or I tried to sound tough, anyway. There was a whole lot more quavering and cracking in my voice than I had planned on.

"That's none of your business. I have every right to be here," he defended himself. "You, on the other hand, I have never seen before. I think you're the one with the explaining to do."

"Do you even know the name of the family who lives here?" I asked boldly.

"Of course. The McCormicks. Patricia and Tim are my aunt and uncle." He rolled the chip bag closed and then licked salt off a few fingers.

"Oh." I relaxed some. "They gave you a key?"

"It's still not any of your business, but I happen to know where they keep their spare key," he said. "On my way to class this morning, my car broke down. I tried to fix it—" he gestured to the dirt scattered across his body—"but I'm really not any good with cars. Since I was close to their house, I decided to stop in and wait here until I could get someone to come give me a ride.

"Wait, why am *I* doing all the talking? *I'm* the one who's allowed to be here. I have no clue who *you* are."

"I have every right to be here, too," I responded quickly.

"I'm Candace's friend from college. I'm staying with her for the summer."

"Is Candy here right now?" he asked eagerly. "Dude, I haven't seen her in so long."

"No, she has class right now." I jumped to attention. "Shoot! Class! I have to leave!"

"What time does it start?" He looked at his watch.

"Ten." I was already halfway up the stairs to grab my purse from the guest bedroom.

"It's 10:15 now," he yelled after me. "You should just ditch."

"It's not like it's an hour-long class!" I called back. "I'm supposed to be there for four hours today!"

"How many times have you skipped so far?" he asked.

"Zero."

"Then you can definitely skip today."

I paused in my run back down the stairs, purse slung over my shoulder, shoes and car keys clenched in my hand. "Well, I guess they did say we could miss a couple of days." But what was I going to do all day, then? Hang out with this guy?

Apparently he had already thought about this dilemma. "If you'll help me get my car situation straightened out, I'll buy you lunch," he offered, crossing his arms and lifting an eyebrow in a bargaining pose. A streak of grease ran from his right elbow to his wrist, drawing my attention to the heavily-muscled biceps peeking out from the sleeves of his T-shirt.

"I don't know anything about cars," I replied.

"I didn't figure you did." He grinned. "But I'm going to need a ride to the repair shop, etcetera, etcetera."

I thought for a minute. I wasn't supposed to take a test today or anything. "Okay. Sounds good."

"Sweet!" He turned back toward the kitchen and lifted up the chip bag. "Let me set this down, and then we can go. And, by the way…" he trailed off, staring at my forehead. "You might want to look in a mirror briefly."

Offended but curious, I raised my free hand and attempted to brush some strands of hair away from my face. They seemed to be slightly stuck. *Crap.* I still had a blob of foundation chilling on my face, junking up the ends of the hair that had swept into it in my haste to get myself together for class. I blushed. "Forgot that was there because *someone* freaked me out. I'm going to need a couple of minutes."

"Okay." He shrugged, then narrowed his eyes. "What's your name?"

"Grace."

"I'm Jake." He smiled. "I'm glad we ran into each other like this, Grace. It's nice to meet you."

CHAPTER THREE

Four years after meeting Jake

"Candace! You're backing out on me now?" I gripped the kitchen counter, staring wide-eyed at the atlas spread out in front of me. "I—I can't—"

"Let me explain." The strain in her voice was suddenly clear, and I began to feel a little bit like a jerk. "It's only because it's an absolute emergency. My grandpa was in a car accident, and things aren't going so well. He's in intensive care right now, and my mom really needs me here to support her. He'll probably end up being fine, but we don't really know."

"Oh, Candace, I'm so sorry. I didn't realize..." Of course I should have known that she would have a good reason. Everything in my life had just been so complicated lately; I was having a difficult time looking beyond my own problems.

"Hold up, I'm not finished." She sucked in a deep breath, like she was about to give me more bad news and needed to summon some courage. "You aren't going to have to go alone. I've found someone else to replace me."

"Oh, Candace, that's great!" I must have misinterpreted her deep breath. This wasn't bad news at all. I would have much preferred that Candace be my traveling buddy, of course, but as long as I didn't have to figure all of this out on my own, I was satisfied. "Thank you. Is it someone I've met before?"

"Umm...yeah." Her voice still sounded plagued with bad news. It had to be because she was upset about her grandfather. "Hey, I've gotta go. I'll talk to you later, all right?"

"Okay. I'm sorry about your grandpa."

"Thanks."

I hung up the phone and tugged my to-do list closer. A lot had changed in the past couple of weeks. Something we had feared might be approaching had come true. As the nation's economy slowly plummeted, the government had been looking for more ways to bring in cash. Gradually, the best, fastest-acting natural products, such as comfrey tea (which could make a cold disappear within a few hours), vanished from the store shelves in what we believed to be a conspiracy to push Americans toward expensive pharmaceutical medications. Over recent months, investigators had been digging deep into medical files, uncovering cases in which it was easy, but not necessarily accurate, to blame deaths on alternative health treatments. I was becoming more and more convinced that the government *wanted* to keep the people sick, wanted to keep them pumping their money into the drug companies, buying medications to cover up the side effects from their other medications. Whether that conspiracy theory was true or not, the government had decided for some reason that the only safe option for Americans was traditional medicine.

Back in the sixties, a group called Codex Alimentarius was created to monitor supplements and food. A few years ago, Codex Alimentarius had taken over Europe to the extent that people could not obtain vitamins and herbs without a prescription, and even then the prices were drastically hiked. The pharmaceutical companies liked the way that this vitamin restriction improved their income so much that two years later, vitamins and herbs were completely outlawed. After much lobbying on both sides and feeling completely overwhelmed by the United States' debt, the U. S. president had signed a law named *Codex Alimentarius Americana*, making my profession illegal, along with the careers of most others associated with alternative health. It was rumored that the pharmaceutical companies had bribed the president into signing this law by promising to pay a large cut of their next five years' income toward the national debt. With this law in effect, no one could purchase supplements, including homeopathic remedies, vitamins, various herbal concoctions, topical ointments for poor skin conditions made out of "natural" ingredients, etcetera, from inside the United States. Anyone who provided these products for others was breaking the law; also, anyone who offered services promoting alternative health options was breaking the law. The government would, of course, have to pass this law just when my supply of some of my favorite products was getting low.

Before *Codex Alimentarius Americana* went into effect, I had been following the news closely for weeks, months even, up until that point, hoping that it wouldn't happen. I had been emailing back and forth with a bioenergetic practitioner in Germany who had been dealing with Codex regulations for years now and was trying to soak up as many tips as I could about keeping my business under wraps and devising ways to work around the law. Strangely enough, I lost correspondence with this man a week before Codex took over in America, and I had to wonder if he, despite all of his precautions, had been caught and imprisoned. As the weeks passed without replies to my emails, I was forced to assume that this was true, and it made me even more nervous about continuing my own practice. I had several late-night discussions with Candace on this topic, and she and I eventually decided that we were going to stick with our jobs. To be bioenergetic practitioners was our calling, if we could be so bold as to label it that. Our careers made us feel fulfilled as people, and we were able to help other people fulfill their lives by giving them the means to energy and good health. We had to fight this thing out until the end.

Consequently, my new life as an undercover bioenergetic practitioner was about to include smuggling products in from Canada and Mexico, where Codex had yet to take effect. An acquaintance of mine from college, Sean Braxton, was the current top smuggler to the eastern half of the United States, and we had set up an appointment with him for our first supplement pick-up. I was terrified, but knowing Candace was going with me had helped to curb my anxiety. The thought of doing this first trip alone had nearly made me pass out. At least Candace had found someone to take her place; it didn't matter who it was—I could get along with anyone for the forty-eight hours necessary to complete the mission.

# # #

I realized as I was packing my bags that Candace had never told me whether the person going with me was just planning to meet at my house, or if I was supposed to meet the person at his or her house, or what was going on. I thought about calling Candace to find out but hated to bother her with anything less than an emergency. Candace and I had originally planned to leave Saturday at 6 a.m., so I cooperated with that plan by pulling myself out of bed at 4:30, showering and packing all of the last-minute essentials like my toothbrush and makeup bag.

I was ready by 5:50. With the extra time I sat at my kitchen table, drumming the fingers of my left hand restlessly and flipping through a couple of Oprah magazines. The crackle of the pages turning seemed too loud for that time of the morning. As much as I tried, I couldn't concentrate on any particular article. At 6:15 I heard someone pull into my driveway, and I quickly pushed the magazines aside in frustration and switched off the light, hurrying to unlock the front door and pull on some shoes.

I walked outside, eager to greet my traveling companion and assure him or her that yes, this was the correct house. It was still so dark outside, and I had a difficult time seeing inside the black Jeep.

Candace's cousin Jake Pennington stepped out, a hesitant smile on his face.

The smile disappeared from mine.

He glanced away and tugged his baseball cap lower on his forehead. "Long time, no see, Grace." His square jaw, dotted with dark stubble, jutted forward rebelliously.

I cleared my throat and crossed my arms over my chest. "Yeah." A year and a half, actually. I was instantly angry with Candace for selecting Jake to accompany me. I knew she was distracted with her grandpa right now, but there was no excuse for her to forget that forcing me to spend an excessive amount of time in a very small space with Jake was a horrible idea. I gritted my teeth, certain that I would rather go by myself than suffer through this situation with him.

Jake answered my unspoken question. "Candace tried to get a couple of other people to go with you, but they had plans this weekend. I need to pick up some stuff for my business, anyway, so it makes sense for me to go with you." During that very first lunch date with Jake so long ago he had shared that he was in his third year of earning a degree in applied kinesiology. Applied kinesiology combines typical chiropractic techniques with muscle-testing, which help the kinesiologist to determine what is physically wrong with the patient as well as to decide what supplements to give the patient. The kinesiologist bases his or her decisions on how strong the patient's extended arm or leg is while focusing pressure on a certain area of the body, like the liver or gallbladder, or how strong the arm or leg is while holding onto the supplement in question. I knew from Candace that Jake had recently begun renting space in a chiropractor's office, but other than that, I hadn't kept up with his life.

I stared at him. "I guess so." There was an awkward pause in which Jake pulled a weed from my yard and I squashed a spider with the toe of my tennis shoe. "You know, I really appreciate your coming and all, but I understand if you don't want to go. I can probably handle this by myself." I tried not to think about my tendency to get lost when traveling even an hour away from home or the fact that if I were all alone I would have even more time to worry about getting caught.

His grin returned, appearing to read my mind. He knew me too well. I used to love it, but today I hated it. "Yeah, right. You'll end up in Houston instead of Quebec."

I rolled my eyes but couldn't help smiling just a little. "It's always a possibility."

"So are we taking your car or my Jeep?"

I sighed, giving in. Despite my aversion to his company, I couldn't stand the thought of making this trip alone. "Let's take my car. I've already got it packed up and full of gas."

He hefted a suitcase out of his passenger seat. "Let's get on the road."

# # #

"We should take a road trip this weekend." I was about to snap from the tension induced by studying for our most recent huge exam. I looked at Jake and Candace, pleading silently for them to please agree to my spontaneous plan. Candace's eyes were suddenly filled with excitement at the prospect of getting away from it all for a few days, but even so, I could tell that she was probably going to say no. Jake, on the other hand, perked up at the idea of procrastination.

I still had four chunky chapters to read through, not to mention all of the reviewing I would need to do in order to be prepared for the test on Tuesday, but I didn't care. Jake also had a large test to prepare for for the following week.

"Where would we go?" he asked eagerly. He closed his text-

book and pushed it aside, along with his half-filled-out study guide.

"Six Flags…Sea World…a zoo…anything that's not home-work," I suggested. "And I feel the need to be away for at least twenty-four hours, preferably the entire weekend."

Jake nodded. I could tell he was contemplating our options.

"You guys, I don't have time for this. I HAVE to study this weekend. I've hardly done anything that I should have this week," Candace said.

Jake glanced over at me and smiled, and I couldn't help but grin back. A lot of my study time had been taken up with talking to him. We frequently stayed up until 1 or 2 in the morning, discussing random likes and dislikes while sitting out on the McCormicks' deck, watching shooting stars. Within the ten days since I'd met him, Jake had started coming over more and more, eating dinner with Candace's family every other day, going to movies with Candace and me, and playing board games with us when we couldn't stand to do homework any longer. I had never seen him actually do home-work until today, even though he always talked about how much he needed to do. He even helped us weed Candace's mom's large flowerbed one Saturday.

# # #

In the seat beside me, Jake started to snore loudly. My map was spread out across his lap, its edges curling up toward the gray ceiling of the car. We had been driving for an hour and a half, and after five minutes of stilted small talk, we somehow reached an agreement to be quiet without ever verbalizing the idea. I had turned up the radio, Jake had scanned through until he'd found a station he wanted to listen to, and that was that. The rest of the time I squinted at the road, wishing I'd remembered my sunglasses, and Jake studied the route I had highlighted. One time I heard a sharp intake of breath as though he wanted to say something, but I pretended I hadn't noticed and turned the radio up even louder, bobbing my head along as though it were one of my favorite songs. I sped toward our destination as much as I dared, willing this trip to end as quickly as possible. I could then return to avoiding contact with Jake. My anger at Candace flickered every ten minutes or so, and I wondered how hard she had really tried to find someone other than Jake to accompany me.

I didn't even offer to stop somewhere for a sit-down lunch or supper. I simply stated, "Burger King sounds kind of good. Is that okay with you?" for lunch and then "How about Arby's?" for supper. He nodded, and we went through the drive-through for both. Each time we stopped to use the restroom, there were never any typical traveling comments, such as "It feels good to stretch," or "It's such a nice day out." We merely went our separate ways and joined back up at the car later. At first I could tell it bothered Jake that we weren't talking, but he seemed to get used to it. I definitely wasn't ready to talk to him, and I probably wouldn't be at any point during this trip.

The "Quebec" that we were going to wasn't actually the Quebec in Canada. It was in North Carolina. Up until last Friday, I had thought that Candace and I were going to have to go to Canada, but she received a call from Sean saying that he was making a trip to North Carolina, and we could meet him there instead if we preferred. I definitely preferred that option, because I had realized too late in the game (last Thursday, in fact) that I needed a passport or at least an enhanced driver's license in order to be able to cross back and forth between the States and Canada. The tricky part of this situation was that if Sean felt at all threatened, he would retreat and we would be unable to pick up our order. And then I would have to go to Canada after all, after waiting a few weeks for my passport to process. We were tentatively supposed to meet with him tomorrow at 3 p.m., but he could change the schedule at any time. He had several other clients that he was meeting with to deliver their products as well and was trying to meet at different locations with each so as to decrease his risk of raising suspicion. He wasn't even going to tell me where to meet him until an hour before our appointment. There was a strong chance that we would have to travel out of the country for all future supplement transfers, and I did not look forward to making an even longer trip than this North Carolina jaunt every couple of months.

# # #

After much debate, we had decided that our road trip would consist of visiting as many Denny's restaurants as possible. As boring and weird as it sounded at first, I soon found that it was the best vacation I'd ever taken. We each packed a bag with enough clothes to last us one overnight stay at a hotel and left at 11:00 that night, driving south out of Michigan with no particular destination in mind other than to stop at whatever Denny's we came across first.

Jake drove Candace's car, while Candace studied by flashlight in the backseat and I kept him company in the front seat. I had packed homework, too, but took my time pulling it out. Jake had

decided not to pack any textbooks, but Candace, ever the responsible
one, had secretly tucked one of his most important books into her
backpack in case he had test-panic later.

We reached our first destination within forty-five minutes.
Having stayed up far too late the night before wasting time on Face-
book, Candace yawned her way out of the car, optimistically bringing
her bookbag inside with her. Jake was nearly jumping with excite-
ment, but that was his typical attitude toward life. I was eager to
spend some time with these people outside of school and home, and so
I did not take any books inside with me. I wasn't hungry at all, but
one of the rules Jake had created for us was that we each had to order
something more than just water at every single one of the restaurants.

# # #

As we crossed over into North Carolina, I conceded that
I finally needed to talk to Jake. It was time to stop for the night,
and Candace and I had booked a couple of hotel rooms days
ago, but now that I was off the expressway and was going to need
to pass through some small towns, I was unsure what direction
to go. Jake had long ago folded up the map and stuck it in the
pocket of his door, and I had prided myself on defeating his
assumption that I would get lost without him. So far I had not
needed him, and I wished that he really had stayed behind in
Michigan. Now, however, with the darkness clouding the street
signs and my contacts becoming dry and fuzzy, I realized that
I would have to concede that I needed his help. I vowed that I
would ask him for as few things as possible during the remainder
of the trip, but for right now, if we were ever going to be able to

get some rest, I would have to actually talk to him. Grrrrr.

"Jake?" I asked hesitantly.

He closed the pamphlet he had been reading. "What?"

"I'm pretty sure we're within half an hour of getting to the hotel where Candace and I had planned to stay. Could you…will you help me figure out how to get there on the map?"

I could see his struggle to hold back the victorious grin that desperately wanted to creep out on his face. "Sure."

CHAPTER FOUR

There were only a few vehicles in the Holiday Inn parking lot. The sunset was full of pinks and purples, and it would have been kind of romantic had I been in that sort of mood, but I was far from it. Seagulls squawked at us and circled above as we silently climbed out of the car. In order to communicate directions, Jake and I had talked a little, but every time he tried to ask me about something personal—something unrelated to figuring out the map—I avoided the question and pointedly stared down at the map, quickly coming up with a topic related to the side streets of North Carolina. There was absolutely no point in trying to be friends with him during the next day or so. I was planning to spend the rest of my life as far from him as I could get, so why bother to make conversation when it was going to mean nothing later? This trip benefited us both because we both needed supplies for our businesses, but anything beyond the business side of it was completely irrelevant. As soon as Candace's fear for her grandpa's life was over, she was definitely going to get an earful from me.

Jake, always a gentleman, assisted me by carrying my bags into the hotel. I checked us in while he milled around the lobby, studying a painting of some flowers, then a vase of some real flowers; next he touched the fabric of the couch and the bumpy texture of the base of a lamp. I'd forgotten how much Jake resembled a little kid when it came to new surroundings. His enthusiasm for life extended into an almost-ADHD type of energy. I refused to be taken in by his positive attitude this time. I rolled my eyes at his curiosity and signed the credit card receipt, accepting with a tight, polite smile the two keys that the clerk handed over.

"Come on, Jake," I said flatly, resisting the urge to mock him by patting my thighs and calling out, "Here, boy!" like one would to an errant dog. I knew my attitude was horrible, but he deserved every minute of it.

# # #

I ordered a simple side salad at that first Denny's. Candace only ordered orange juice, but Jake ordered a breakfast large enough for two people, with three plates overflowing with pancakes, toast, sausage, eggs, and hashbrowns. I watched, amused, as he dug into it all. Candace sipped on her orange juice while highlighting key terms, occasionally jabbing a sarcastic retort into the conversation.

Around 1:30 we decided to head for a new location. Candace and I left Jake to guard our purses and her backpack while we wisely used the restroom, uncertain how long we would be in the car this next time. Upon our return, which was fewer than five minutes after we had left the table, I was surprised to see Jake's head tipped back against the top of the booth cushion, his mouth open and eyes closed. He had seemed too full of energy to fall asleep so easily.

"Wake up, Jake," I said, shaking his shoulder. He woke up quickly, rubbed his eyes, and jumped to his feet.

"Let's get out of here," he said, straightening his shirt and grabbing his wallet out of his back pocket.

I was about to suggest that maybe we should find a hotel for the night, all get some sleep, and restart this journey in a few hours. Candace spoke before I had the chance, though.

"Jake…where's my backpack?" she asked carefully, worry bordering her tone.

"Huh?" He looked under the table, then at both benches of the booth. "I…uh…"

"We asked you to watch our stuff, Jake," Candace exclaimed. "We were gone for, like, three minutes. If you're so tired, why didn't you just say so? I don't know why we didn't just wait and leave in the morning anyway."

I opened my purse and was relieved to see that my wallet was still inside. Candace must have followed my same train of thought because she checked her own purse as soon as I closed mine, and I saw her relax somewhat when she found what she was looking for. She glanced under the table one more time, and her eyebrows pinched together worriedly again. "I'm going to go ask the hostess if she saw anyone leave with a backpack," she said, spinning around and heading for the front of the restaurant.

"The semester's almost over," Jake grumbled, trying to assuage his own guilt. "How much more is she going to need those books, anyway?"

"Jake, she put one of your textbooks in there, too," I replied *quietly and listed the name of it.*

He paled and tightened his fist around his wallet. "We've got to find that backpack," he stated with renewed conviction. He placed a few dollars on the table for a tip and joined Candace in her interview with the hostess.

I gripped my purse more tightly to my body and began to walk carefully around the dining area, failing in my attempt to look casual while I peered under tables. I hoped that whoever had taken it had looked inside before he or she got too far and discarded it once the realization hit that homework was there but nothing else.

# # #

I lay on my left side in the unfamiliar hotel bed, the chemicals that the maid had cleaned with earlier in the day dancing a faint burning scent into my nostrils. Orange-tinged light from the parking lot sneaked in around the edges of the curtain, while someone's love for Rascal Flatts drifted in through the glass in the form of "Mayberry" cranked to full volume and supplemented by raucous, off-key singing. Every few seconds there was loud laughter from the neighbors on the right side of my room, and if I listened carefully enough, I could hear bits of the TV program Jake was watching in the rented room to my left. It was just 9:00, and normally I went to bed at this time because I had to get up so early for my business, but at this point I felt as though I could stay up for several more hours.

The scratchy, floral bedspread twitched as I shifted, and the feel of it against my neck made me grimace. I tossed it aside, pulled the sheet up further, and then brought the bedspread and blankets up again, folding the top down so that they would be nowhere near my neck. I had just settled down once more when Jake knocked on the door connecting our two rooms.

Huffing angrily, I threw on my bathrobe and pulled the door open.

"Hey, Grace," he said casually, appearing not to notice that I was disgruntled at being disturbed. "Could I borrow your car to go get something to eat? Or do you want to come with me?"

"I'm not hungry. How much more junk food do you need?" I meant it to sound annoyed, but he thought I was joking and gave a short laugh.

"I just want a shake or something. Trust me, I have drastically improved my eating habits since college, but I always eat whatever I want when it comes to road trips." He smiled pleadingly, holding out his hand for car keys.

I grabbed my keychain off the dresser and handed it over. "I don't want anything. Thanks, though."

He nodded and didn't protest when I nudged the door shut again.

It took me two hours after that to fall asleep. In the midst of all my bitterness, I must have forgotten to set my alarm, because Jake pounded on the door at 7:30, and I was still in bed, out cold and unaware of the time.

"Grace? Are you ready to go?" he asked tentatively.

I glanced at the digital clock and cursed, repeating last night by throwing on my bathrobe and opening the door to a happy Jake.

His shoulders sank a little when he saw that I wasn't

ready. "I guess you overslept, huh? That's all right. I'll go get some breakfast for us both and leave you to get dressed and all." He was the one to close the door this time. I never even said anything.

I grabbed my phone charger to plug it in while I showered and suddenly noticed that I had a missed call.

Oh, no…oh, no. It was Sean Braxton. He had called me twenty minutes ago, and I had not answered.

I hurriedly called him back, running my fingers through my hair frantically, scared that he had changed my appointment slot and that somehow I would be unable to pick up my load now. Not only would that make all this time spent with Jake completely unnecessary, but also I would not be able to run my business for potentially several weeks at a time. It did not do any good to test clients and then not be able to supply them with what they needed to improve their health.

"Hello?"

"Sean! I am so sorry I missed your call. My alarm didn't go off, and I accidentally left my phone on vibrate, and…"

"It's fine. I'm changing your appointment time to 10:00," he said calmly. Sean never freaked out about anything. He was almost like a hypnotist or something.

"Today?" I asked, my voice squeaking.

"Yes, this morning. Can you still make it?"

"Where are we meeting?" It was 7:42. There was a chance that even if Jake and I left now, we'd never be able to make it to wherever Sean had in mind.

"A Barnes and Noble just outside of Quebec." He gave me an address and the phone number for the Barnes and Noble in case we got lost.

"Sean, we'll do our best to make it. I'm not sure how far that is from here." I pulled clothes from my suitcase as we talked. "Okay?"

"Okay. If you can't make it, I probably won't have anything else open unless someone cancels last-minute."

"All right." I tried to sound confident, tried to make myself believe that of course we would get there in time. It was all going to work out.

I managed to shower and wash my hair in five minutes, pulling on clean clothes while my body was still half-wet. I pulled my dripping hair into a ponytail underneath a base-ball cap and applied the bare minimum of makeup that I felt I needed. The night before I hadn't removed much from my suit-case, so re-packing it was easy. I was pulling on my jacket when Jake knocked at the door.

"Whoa, you're ready to go?" he asked. "I thought it would take you, like, you know, an hour or so." He held up a plate with a bagel and cream cheese on it and a plastic cup of orange juice. "Slim pickings on the continental breakfast. Here you go."

"Sean Braxton, the supplier, called me a little bit ago," I explained in a rush. "We have to get going *now*. He changed our appointment. We're meeting with him in less than two hours."

"What?! Where?!" Jake shoved the food at me and ran over to his bed to zip up his suitcase.

"A Barnes and Noble near Quebec. I'm not even sure how close we are to Quebec right now."

He stopped abruptly, a relaxed smile on his face. "Oh, we'll be fine then. I was just talking to one of the hotel clerks while I was downstairs, and she was saying that she lives in Quebec. If she drives here for work every day, it can't be that far. We must be within an hour."

"Let's hope so. Get your stuff, and let's check out."

Jake drove so that I could eat in the car. We stopped at a gas station across the street and then used Jake's laptop to get directions on MapQuest to the bookstore. I was pleased to discover that it should only take us forty-five minutes to get there, as long as nothing went wrong. We even had a little bit of time to spare in case we became lost.

Now that everything was coming together, I was feeling a little friendlier toward Jake, and I even made an effort to start a conversation about something other than the matter at hand. Today, though, he seemed to be the one who didn't want to talk.

"So, how's your business going? Has your number of clients decreased at all since that stupid law passed?"

"It's going okay. About the same number of clients." He clenched his jaw, staring intently at the road ahead.

"That's, uh, good." Ah, well. I deserved this after how I'd treated him the past twenty-four hours. *Whatever.*

"Do you hear that?" he asked suddenly.

"What?"

"That…clicking."

"No." My car was only two years old, and I had had the oil changed and the brakes checked and everything a couple of days before this trip. *He must be imagining things. Or trying to get back at me for treating him so crappy yesterday.*

I leaned a little closer to him to get a look at the dash-board. The temperature of the engine was far too hot. "Jake,

I think it's overheating or something. Maybe you should pull over."

He studied the dashboard in between glances at the traffic in front of him. "Okay, find me a good spot to pull over, and I will."

We were in the middle lane of a three-lane expressway, and everyone must have been on the way to their offices because we were surrounded by men and women, clutching Starbucks cups, in business suits and expensive vehicles. I looked at the side mirror and then twisted to check the blind spot, my neck aching with the strain. Maybe I really would need to start being nicer to Jake so that he would be willing to give me a free chiropractic adjustment before all of this was over.

"Okay, you can get over," I said, still not too concerned about our predicament. "Hey, there's an exit. Let's just get off the expressway there, and we can stop in a parking lot somewhere and try to figure out what's going on." I pointed at the green sign ahead.

Suddenly the air was filled with the sound of horns honking, effectively drowning out the eighties' music we were listening to.

"What's going on?" I asked, looking over at Jake.

He was staring straight ahead, eyes wide. I followed his gaze and screamed.

"It's on fire! PULL OVER NOW!"

# # #

"You know, I did just see two teen boys walk out with a backpack," the hostess said, her eyebrows knotted together in concentration. "They left probably two minutes ago."

Jake scurried for the door.

Candace looked over at me, confused as to why Jake was suddenly so involved in the search, and then followed him out the door. I handed over enough cash to cover our bill before joining Candace.

"He found out that one of his books is in there, too," I explained once we were out in the parking lot.

"This has to be the only time in my life when bringing homework along with me was not a good idea," Candace complained.

Jake was running through the dark lot, looking frantically inside of cars, and in general appeared to be insane. He whipped past two women near our age who were stumbling a bit as they walked, presumably headed into Denny's to sober up before attempting to drive home.

"Is it just me, or is the world moving really fast right now?" I heard one of the girls ask the other.

"I think I found them!" Jake yelled, covering up the answer to the question.

Candace and I started toward him. I was astonished that he had been able to solve this mystery in such a quick manner. By the time we had reached him, though, he was shaking his head and walking back toward us, shoulders slumped. "False alarm. I saw two guys' heads in a truck and assumed that it was them. It's actually two old men. They're out cold, probably drunk."

Candace sighed. "I'm going to have to buy new textbooks, guys. This stinks."

"Wait a minute!" I said, peering past Jake to Denny's driveway, where two kids, one wearing a backpack, sat impatiently on their bikes, looking for an opportunity to cross the street. "Candace, do you think that's your backpack?"

She squinted. "It's too dark to tell for sure, but it might be. That one seems to have a lot of stuff in it, like mine did. I'll go get the car. Maybe we can follow them a little, try to figure out if it's mine or not before confronting them."

Jake was already running after the boys. He must really need to do well on this test, I thought.

They heard his pounding footsteps and, after a quick look both ways to see if they could make it across without getting smashed, pedaled as fast as they could to the sidewalk on the other side of the street. Jake just kept tracking them.

Candace and I ducked into her car and were soon driving parallel with the boys on a slow-speed chase. Jake was so focused on the boys that he didn't seem to notice us. Candace, after realizing that it really was her backpack, rolled down her window and called out, "You guys need to stop right now or we're calling the police!"

They barely glanced at us and just pedaled faster, although one of the boys, while watching straight in front of him, did lift up his hand and flip us off.

Candace huffed and gritted her teeth. "We will get my backpack back, Grace."

Jake was becoming low on energy—he had fallen back quite a ways now, and we ended up pulling into a gas station and picking him up in our car, easily catching up with the boys again.

"Come on, now!" Candace yelled at the boys. "Obviously, we know you guys are the ones who did it! Just give me my bag back, and we won't call the police! There are only textbooks in there, anyway!"

Apparently that was the right thing to say, because they passed under a streetlight and I could see the facial expression on the boy wearing the backpack—it was one of disappointed realization that what he thought was a great find was no treasure at all, but merely the symbol of something he hated. He slowed a little and shifted the bag off one of his shoulders, removing one hand from his handlebars to unzip the backpack and confirm what was inside. "Aw, crap, Joel!" he exclaimed. "They're right! Just stupid books!"

His companion shook his head, resigned. "Whatever, man. Do what you want with it, then."

The first boy shrugged the bag completely off his back and threw it to the ground, increasing his bike's speed as soon as he was free of his burden. Candace screeched to a stop, threw the car into park, and leapt out to rescue her bag, protectively cradling it to her chest once it was in her possession again. The vehicles surrounding us honked, and I leaned over and hit her emergency lights.

"My book's still in there, right?" Jake called tentatively out the window to her as she walked back to the car.

"As if they would decide to take just your reflexology book." Candace rolled her eyes but checked anyway. "Yep. Jake, you're going to be able to pass your test after all."

He laughed. "Oh, I wasn't actually worried about the book. I have plenty of notes back at home that I could study for the test from. I stuck my paycheck in the back of that book a few days ago, though, and forgot to cash it. If those boys found it, they were going to be four hundred dollars richer, and I wouldn't be able to pay a bunch of bills. But, um, I guess I'm glad the book is okay, too."

Candace rolled her eyes and pulled Jake's book out of her bag, handing it to him. "Here. You be in charge of your own book from now on."

CHAPTER FIVE

Jake swept my car over to the rumble strip so quickly that I thought we were flying for a second. He scrambled out of the car, and I unlocked my seatbelt, twisting to grab things that were important to me out of the backseat. Jake had my passenger-side door open within five seconds, pulling on my right arm to drag me away from the car while I resisted, snatching my purse and a bag of important documents with my left hand. I also grabbed the bag that held his laptop, tossing it out the door at him. The air whooshed out of him as his computer slammed him in the gut, and he momentarily released my arm to get a grip on the laptop bag. I scooped up my cell phone from the center console and finally tore the map from the door's side pocket, tumbling out of the vehicle as my car's flames shot higher. Jake had a hold on my arm tight enough to cause bruises as he hauled me away from the scene twenty feet or so.

We were now standing in weeds that crept up to my thighs, flies and bees buzzing around our heads. Jake flipped open his cell phone and dialed 911, but it was unnecessary because there was already a police car pulling over, carefully parking a safe distance from the wild explosion that my poor Grand Prix was about to turn into. I could see that the policewoman was on her radio, calling some help for us.

I dumped all of the stuff in my arms on the ground and flopped down among the weeds, unsure whether I should cry or perhaps beat the earth with my fists.

Jake, standing beside me, looked down at our belongings that I had gathered from the car. "Why did you save the *map*, Grace, of all things?" He gave a strained laugh.

"I don't *know*, Jake! How was I supposed to think clearly? Why can't you just stop pretending that we can still get along, that we can joke like we used to? We both know we don't have that kind of a relationship anymore! So just SHUT UP!" I moaned and buried my face in my palms, bumping the brim of my baseball cap up to make room for my hands. "My car, my *car*! This is awful!"

He didn't respond, and I slowly turned my head up toward him, realizing how harsh I had been. It was too late now to talk about anything personal, though; the policewoman had jogged her way over to us, approaching with intense concentration as she appeared to assess us for injuries. The hurt expression on Jake's face quickly morphed into blank indifference as the stranger joined us.

"Are you guys okay?" the woman asked. She bypassed Jake and came directly to me—she probably thought my reaction to all of my emotional stress was the result of a head injury or something.

I waved her away when she placed a couple of fingers lightly on my wrist. "I'm fine, I'm fine."

She backed off a little, straightening. "The firemen should be here soon. Do either of you have any injuries that need attention?"

We both shook our heads. I felt ashamed of my outburst and regretted the horrible manner in which I'd treated Jake during the past day. I didn't want to talk to this policewoman or to anyone else. What if we'd died in my burning car? I certainly didn't want to leave this life so angry at Jake for something that had happened a long time ago.

"Okay, then, I think maybe we'd better get a little further away from your car," she pressured us, demonstrating what she meant by walking even more out into the weeds that were scratching at my arms and face. "What are your names?" she called over her shoulder.

"Grace," I mumbled, rising reluctantly to my feet and following her, glancing back over my shoulder at my car, now half-eaten by flames. Other vehicles sped past it in the lane closest to the median, and even from here, I could see all of the drivers' heads directed at my dying car, gawking at me and Jake standing practically in the jungle with all of these ridiculous bugs that kept gnawing on my pale skin. I already had several small red bumps covering my arms that had not been there just three minutes prior.

"What?" the policewoman asked.

"I'm Jake, and she's Grace," Jake responded. He walked behind me, and I wished I could make eye contact with him to see how badly I'd hurt him, but at the same time I was scared to do so.

"I'm Chrystina," she said. "Where are you guys headed this morning, anyway?"

I gulped and ran several possible replies through my head.

She looked back when neither of us responded right away, one eyebrow cocked.

Jake helped us look less suspicious by chuckling. "Just to the bookstore. I guess you're going to have to wait to get that book after all, Grace."

I nodded, smiling and shrugging my shoulders, playing along. "Yeah, it's too bad. I've waited for *months* for it to come out."

"Oh, what book?" Chrystina asked.

We all stopped. Chrystina must have decided that we were a sufficient distance away to prevent getting struck by flying car pieces.

I pretended to be studying a caterpillar on the daisy by my feet. "*Walking in the Wilderness* by Jackie Coyote," I improvised.

"Huh. I've never heard of that author before," Chrystina remarked. "I'll have to check out her work sometime."

"Yeah, she's pretty good," I replied, folding my arms across my chest and grimacing at my watch. "Barnes and Noble opens at ten; I was trying to get there when they opened." It was 9:10; I was going to lose my chance to meet with Sean, and because of Chrystina's eavesdropping ears, I couldn't even call him to let him know I wouldn't be there. Sean was always calm, but he wasn't the type to give second chances; I figured I would have to find a new supplier altogether now. When I didn't call and didn't show up, he would probably assume irresponsibility on my part, especially after I missed his call this morning.

Ambulances and police cars swarmed the area all of a sudden, but the people we really needed to be there—the firemen—were nowhere to be found. The police parked their cars sideways across the expressway, effectively blocking traffic from being able to get too close to the fire. It was like a crime scene, except that I hadn't even committed the crime yet. I was a little worried that I might reveal the true reason for our drive this morning if questioned too closely. I had always been a bad liar and was easily pressured into doing things.

"You guys stay here; I'm going to go talk with them," Chrystina said, pointing to the policemen leaning against their sideways-parked cars.

"Call Sean," Jake hissed as soon as she was out of earshot.

I jumped to attention, digging my phone out of my pocket and pulling up Sean's number as quickly as possible. He was the one to miss my call this time.

"Sean, this is Grace, and I'm having some car trouble," I began. "It's 9:15, and my car's on fire right now, literally, and I don't think I'm going to be able to make it to my 10:00 appointment. If there is any way that we can re-schedule, *please* let me know. I'm sorry about this." As I closed my phone, I realized the enormity of my situation—not only was I not going to be able to get to my appointment on time, but I didn't even have a vehicle to transport the goods. I was going to have to rent a car or have someone else drive down from home to give Jake and me a ride. This trip was turning far more expensive than I had planned. Chances were we were going to have to stay another night in a hotel, if not more. I didn't even have any clean clothes; although I had brought along an extra outfit, our suitcases were in the trunk.

More sirens wailed, and the fire trucks pulled up. They were about to douse my car when the thing that I was surprised had not already happened occurred—the huge explosion I had been fearing. Jagged pieces of Grand Prix shot up into the air thirty feet. My lower lip quivered, and my eyes filled with fluid. Heat vibrated through the air all the way over to where Jake and I stood as an ash floated down to rest on my shoulder. Jake reached over and brushed it away; I burst into tears and crumpled to the ground.

CHAPTER SIX

Once we were on the road again, headed to another Denny's (Jake claimed the run had woken him up—that he was good to go for at least two more hours), Candace decided that she needed to sleep. So, covered up with three sweatshirts, she stretched out in the backseat as best she could while seat-belted, and was out within just a couple of minutes.

It was still only 1:30 in the morning, and Jake and I were accustomed to approaching the ends of our late-night discussions around this time, so we were rather awake.

I pressed my head against the window, trying to see constellations. When the reflection from the glow of the dashboard buttons against the glass interfered with my ability to properly view the night sky, I rolled the window down and stuck my head outside. My nose wrinkled when I realized the cold air smelled of gasoline fumes and skunk, but I could see Orion and the Big Dipper a lot better.

Jake laughed, and I pulled myself back inside to frown at him.

"What are you, a dog now?"

"Hey. If I'm a dog, then so are you for running after those kids on their bikes," I informed him playfully.

He punched me lightly in the arm. "Well, since we're both dogs, I guess we should stick together," he said.

And then he leaned over and kissed me.

# # #

Things were wonderfully awkward after our kiss. I wasn't sure what to say, and Jake didn't seem to be sure either, but I reveled in the knowledge that my suspicions were confirmed—he liked me. I wasn't sure what to do with that information—I liked him, but I didn't know how Candace would feel if he and I started dating, and I wasn't even sure if he was someone I wanted to date. Our trio of summer friendship had been beautifully uncomplicated until now, and I wondered whether Candace would feel uncomfortable hanging out with Jake and me if we were a couple. I was really enjoying my friendship with Jake; even though I hadn't known him for very long yet, the friendship I had with him was closer than any I had had in the past with a guy, and I didn't want to lose that. Then I suddenly realized that perhaps I was letting my thoughts run too far away and that maybe the kiss hadn't meant anything to Jake. I was pretty certain, though, that he liked me at least a little bit, and so I clung to that hope, pretending to sleep while rolling it around in my head like an overactive pinball.

The last thing I remembered was Jake turning up the radio, and then I must have actually fallen asleep because the next thing I knew it was 3:00, and we were in the parking lot of the second

Denny's stop. Candace was grumbling groggily from the backseat, saying something about that we could go in without her; she just wanted to sleep.

I pushed through my fog to say, "It's probably not that safe of an idea for you to stay out in the car, Candace. We don't even know what kind of a town we're in." Truthfully, I didn't really want to get out of the car, either. I just wanted to get back to sleep filled with dreams and thoughts of Jake.

"I don't care," she whispered into the sweatshirt pulled up to her chin, nearly back asleep again already.

"Come on, guys, we all have to get something at each Denny's. We can't break the rules on only the second stop." This was the only rule I'd ever seen Jake enforce—usually he was up for breaking rules left and right, like when he urged me to skip class the first day I met him.

"Well, then, take money out of my purse and get me a doggy bag," Candace suggested. "I'm not getting out of the car."

"Fine. I guess we're each allowed to sit out one stop," Jake compromised. "Do you want something to eat or no?"

"No. Stop talking to me," Candace said, unbuckling her seatbelt and sliding further down on the seat, using her purse as a pillow.

I was a little too eager to please Jake, and so I didn't verbally protest going inside with him, although I preferred to return to sleeping as well. I pulled my hair out of my eyes as we walked into the restaurant, forcing it up into a ponytail, hoping that I didn't look quite as bad as I figured I did.

After we had ordered—I just asked for hot tea this time; Jake requested a hot fudge sundae—we sat quietly, looking at each other *nervously. I tore the thin paper from a straw into tiny bits. A waitress walked by quickly, eager to set down her heavy tray, and the swirl of air blew my mountain of shredded paper off the table and onto Jake's sweater. He looked down at the white flakes clinging to his shirt and frowned, and I laughed, the sound startlingly, abnormally loud in the mostly-deserted restaurant. As I attempted to stifle my laugh, it somehow turned into a snort, and I blushed deeply, mortified.*

Jake started laughing as I tucked my chin and grimaced, my eyes begging him just to ignore it. He finally grew silent again, and now the situation was even more awkward than before because both of us had yet to attempt to start a conversation. He connected two drops of water on the table with his finger and then drew squiggles in the condensation on his water glass, squinting in concentration. I could tell he was working up to saying something important, and I did my best not to look at him, trying not to pressure him into anything.

Jake cleared his throat. "In the car, I'm sorry, I probably shouldn't have—"

"It's fine," I said quickly.

Everything was quiet again. I sipped at my water and looked everywhere but into Jake's eyes. He flicked crumbs off the table. The waitress brought my tea and Jake's sundae, seemed to pick up on the awkward vibes, and backed away from the table without saying anything.

"How is it?" I asked after he had taken a couple of bites.

Jake apparently didn't notice that I had motioned to his ice cream and looked at me strangely, a grin creeping out at the same time. "It's great," he said, staring at my lips.

I snickered.

"Should we—" his voice cracked, and he smiled again,

embarrassed—*"Do you want to talk about this or no?"*

Considering there was a slight possibility that he was going to tell me he just hadn't been thinking clearly—that the kiss had been a case of poor, exhausted judgment—I was unsure whether I wanted to talk about it or not. If we discussed it now, at 3:00 in the morning at Denny's, while both of us were already high-strung from the backpack chase and little sleep, it might all come out wrong. Plus, either outcome might make the rest of the trip awkward for Candace. I still had doubts about how she would feel regarding all of this.

"What if we…wait…until next week, when we're back at home?" I said carefully. "I don't think now is the best time."

He nodded thoughtfully. "Yeah, I'd say you're probably right about that." He looked relieved at having more time to think about what he was going to say, and I certainly felt that way, too.

The rest of our Denny's trip was not nearly as adrenaline-inducing as that first night. All in all, we stopped at nine different Denny's, and Jake ate all sorts of fattening, sugary foods at every single location. Candace's mood was much improved once we stopped at a hotel and all got some sleep, and she seemed to be unaware of all of the meaningful glances between Jake and me and the way he seemed to touch me more than usual—a hand on the shoulder here, hand cupping the small of my back there.

I tried to follow Candace's example and study a couple of different times, but I just couldn't concentrate. Until Jake and I had our talk, I was probably going to do poorly on my schoolwork. I came to terms with that idea quickly. So far I had earned As and Bs on everything important, so one bad test grade and maybe a couple of poor grades on some small papers shouldn't affect anything too much.

Monday night, once Candace was in bed, Jake invited me

to go on a walk with him. One part of me wanted to prolong this occasion, while the other part just wanted to get everything out in the open, even if he was going to tell me he wasn't interested in me. The end of the summer was merely three weeks away, so even if we did arrange some sort of dating relationship, there was no guarantee that it would last beyond those three weeks, as we would be living a couple of hours apart. I had always been bad at keeping in touch with people who moved away, so I did not have much hope for a long-distance relationship.

Our walk and conversation were brief. Jake expressed that he was interested in me, but that he didn't want to damage our friendship, and I agreed with him. We decided that we would keep things low-key for the next three weeks, try to spend more time together just the two of us (yet also try not to weird Candace out), and see what happened. I was satisfied with that answer—a little disappointed (what girl doesn't want a bigger commitment than that?), but I knew it was the best option.

He kissed me before I went into the house, and, with that happy ending, I decided that I might finally be able to study a little for my test that was coming up the next day. I was sad to see him drive home, but I looked forward to the date he had promised me we would go on Thursday night.

# # #

As I drove home to spend some time with my parents at the end of the semester, I reflected on the most recent days with Jake. While repeatedly blasting Puddle of Mudd's "Psycho" and Alien Ant Farm's "Smooth Criminal" (my two favorite songs at the time), I remembered all of the kisses, all of the small gifts Jake had bought me, and all of the great conversations we had had. Jake had told me to call him once I arrived at home, and, illustrating his quirky sense of humor, had handed over a balloon to remind me to call him. So now the ridiculous Mylar SpongeBob balloon bounced around in my backseat, partially blocking my view out the back window. Jake knew that I hated SpongeBob, and when I voiced aloud why in the world would he buy me a symbol of something I hated to remind me of himself, he simply shrugged and grinned. "I just saw it and thought of you," he explained, then teased, "Isn't it great?"

"Fantastic." I had rolled my eyes and despised the balloon even as I loved it simply because it was from him.

Now it was probably going to be two months before I would see him again. We would each be starting a new semester in a couple of weeks, and I had been able to find a school near my home that provided bioenergetic classes, so I would no longer be imposing on Candace's family. Jake was driving out west to visit a friend and would return to his home the day before his new classes would begin.

Against all odds, our relationship progressed as we talked on the phone nearly every day and visited each other during school breaks over the next year. Finally, summer arrived again, and before I would have to start summer classes, I planned a two-week trip out to Candace's home to visit both Candace and Jake. Candace had been aware of mine and Jake's relationship for quite some time now, of course, and was surprisingly supportive.

On the last day of the two weeks, Jake and I took a walk, reminiscent of our walk from about nine months earlier. I was sad that we probably wouldn't see each other for another three months again, and was, in fact, contemplating breaking up with him just

*because it added a lot of stress to my life to have a long-distance rela-
tionship. Since I was taking summer classes again, I only had one more
semester after that summer, and then I would be able to open my own
business. I knew that my bioenergetic business was going to be a lot of
work, and I didn't want to be distracted by a relationship that probably wasn't going to work out anyway. I was twenty-three; Jake was
almost twenty-two. We were young and both about to start businesses
that would take up the majority of our time; we didn't need to lose
sleep over a relationship that mostly consisted of phone conversations.*

*In preparation for this last day spent with Jake, I had prac-
ticed over and over again what I was going to say—"Jake, I've
enjoyed getting to know you, but I don't think it's the best idea for
us to continue our relationship. We're both about to get much busier,
and being weighed down by a long-distance relationship is only
going to take important time away from developing our careers. I
don't know if we can return to just a friendship, but I would like to
try." It was the best I could come up with. I had practiced it in front
of Candace a couple of times, who urged me not to break up with
Jake, but I knew it was the right thing to do.*

*As we rounded the corner onto another street, a bored, over-
protective dog barked, pulling at his tether in an effort to intimidate
us. The wind blew stronger, and I shivered, despite the heavy sweatshirt I wore with a tank top and T-shirt layered beneath. Goose-
bumps rose on my arms, partly from the chill and partly from dread
at what I was about to do. For all I knew, Jake wanted to break
up with me, too, but otherwise, in this relationship that was going
rather well, what I was about to say would be a total surprise. We
hardly ever even argued over anything, and when we did, it was
stupid stuff that was easily resolved.*

I took a deep breath and slowed my pace, turning to face him. Strangely, he looked just as nervous as I felt, and I wondered if maybe he was going to break up with me. Could it be that easy? Could we just mutually decide that it was best for us to break up with no anger or tears involved? Maybe we could go back to being friends after all. I was instantly more comfortable and decided just to get it over with. "Jake, I've enjoyed getting to know—"

At the same time he said, "Grace, I have something really important to tell you."

Up until now, it had been several minutes since either of us had spoken, and so the fact that all of a sudden we both had something to say made us laugh a little.

"Go ahead," I told him.

"Okay." He looked unbelievably pale in the moonlight, almost as though he were about to get sick. "Could you just stop a minute?" he asked, not in an impolite way, but I recognized that whatever he was about to tell me was extremely serious, so I obeyed. Here it comes, I thought, and nearly smiled at the realization that I wasn't even going to have to use the speech I had prepared.

I gave him my full attention and grew lightheaded when he dropped to one knee.

"Grace, I've really enjoyed getting to know you the past several months."

Hey, that's my line.

"I know we haven't been able to spend a lot of time together, but through our phone conversations and the small amount of time we have spent together, I've only found myself wanting more. Candace, who has spent much more time with you than I have, only speaks highly of you, and you and I have such similar goals—to *start our own health practices. Our lives seem to overlap so well with each other, and I can't get enough of you. Grace, I love you. Will you marry me?" He pulled a small velvet jewelry box out of his jacket pocket and opened it to show me a diamond ring.*

I tried to swallow and choked on my own spit. I was grateful that the coughing fit which ensued gave me a few moments to gather my thoughts. I had been planning to break up with him, but I had no good reasons for it other than that I thought we weren't going to have enough time for each other anymore. We got along really well; he took good care of me and made me laugh. It was true, we did have a similar goal to each start our own health practice. Maybe it was a sign. Maybe we weren't supposed to break up but instead marry each other. If we were married, we wouldn't have the problem of living in separate states and could build one health business together instead of two separate businesses. And I did love him—I really did.

He stared up at me expectantly, looking even closer to puking the longer I made him wait.

"Yes, Jake. I would love to marry you."

CHAPTER SEVEN

Two and a half months passed. We were planning a June wedding, which provided me with about a year to work out all of the details. My last free weekend in August before the new semester I drove down to visit Jake and Candace. I decided to drop in and surprise Jake at his house by cooking him supper while he was at work (he had given me a key to his house a while back).

When I pulled into his driveway, I immediately noticed and was suspicious of a shiny black Cougar parked up close to the house. As I idled in Jake's driveway, a woman hopped out and peered back at me, hovering half inside and half outside the car—probably wondering if I was dangerous. Her long, curly blonde hair flowed down the back of a well-exercised body sporting a short, tight black dress. I didn't recognize her, and she didn't appear to recognize me, either, but once she realized that I was a woman and most likely posed no threat, her posture relaxed, and she closed her car door and waited for me to get out of my car, too.

I tensed up more. What in the world was she doing at Jake's

house? I couldn't get out of my car fast enough to ask that question.
She smiled at me while I spoke. "Hi, who are you?"

"I'm Amber," she replied confidently. "Jake's girlfriend. Are
you his cousin Candace? He always talks about how much fun the
two of you have hanging out together."

I shook my head. My throat seized up, and I wasn't sure if I
was about to cry or if I was going to scream in angry frustration. "No,
um, you know what? I'll stop by later when Jake's here." The thumb
of my left hand, which was hanging down at my side, quickly twisted
the diamond on my ring in toward my palm, and I ducked back into
my car and retreated as fast as I could without hitting Jake's mailbox.
As I passed his mailbox, I wished briefly that I had smashed into it,
but then the grief overcame me and I drove away, large tears falling so
rapidly I thought I just might dehydrate into a raisin. At that moment
I wished I could be a dried grape, sitting in a cardboard box with
other raisins, with the main purpose in life of being eaten. I wondered
if it would hurt to be eaten, and then I decided it didn't matter if it
hurt or not because it would be over in a couple of seconds, whereas
Jake's betrayal would potentially be with me for decades.

# # #

"Hey, now," Jake whispered, squatting down beside me.
"It's going to be okay. We'll track down another car for you and
get the supplements some other way. It's not the end of the
world."

"I—know." I gulped in air between the two words, my
sobs nearly destroying my ability to speak. "I just—I just—I
don't know."

Jake laughed cautiously. "That made no sense."

"Jake, I'm sorry for treating you like crap the last couple of days." There, I'd said it. I still felt as though he deserved to be treated poorly, but I had been overly and unnecessarily cruel. "Thank you for your help." I couldn't really choke anything else out. This was the extent of my goodwill.

He looked ashamed. "Yeah, well, I probably deserve it. Back when the whole situation went down a couple of years ago, I kept making excuses and trying to get you to listen to me, but there really wasn't any excuse for it. I was stupid. I'm sorry, too."

I smiled at him weakly, letting him know I accepted his apology. It felt better to get this all out in the open.

The firemen were covering the shards of my car in arcs of water, and the large flames had shrunk down to much more manageable two-foot waves of orange light. The posture of the people decked out in their protective overalls and bulky jackets was more relaxed than it had been before the explosion, and it seemed that the worst was over. I could get on with the remains of my life.

Chrystina returned to stand by us. "Once all of this has cooled off a little, I can give you guys a ride somewhere, if you'd like." She brushed her bangs out of her face and looked from one to the other of us—a little longer on Jake than on me, I noticed. *Don't even think about it. He's a loser,* I screamed inside my head. Despite the fact that I had somewhat forgiven him, it was going to take him a while to prove to me that he had actually changed. I was still incredibly skeptical. Even though I didn't know this policewoman, she seemed like a good person. I didn't wish some guy to ruin her life. Plus, Jake was a bad match for her, anyway, with his illegal career.

I suddenly wondered why I was thinking about all of this so much and decided to banish it from my head. We were in a completely different state from where either of us lived—nothing was going to become of Chrystina's interest anyway.

"Thanks," I said to her, neither accepting nor rejecting her offer.

Chrystina nodded once.

My cell rang. I glanced at the number, saw that it was Sean, and started to walk away from Chrystina and Jake before I answered it. "Hey, Sean," I said quietly.

I was used to Sean sounding calm and matter-of-fact about things, but he was abnormally excited this time. "Grace! I got your message. Your car's on fire? Do you think it was foul play? Do you think someone's trying to sabotage your trip?"

I laughed at that idea. "I don't think so, Sean. I don't think I have anybody who's quite that angry with me about anything."

"Don't be too sure," he cautioned. "I've seen some weird things happen the last few weeks."

I smiled and shook my head even though he couldn't see me do so. "All right, I'll keep my eyes open for enemies. Is there some other arrangement we can make for the pick-up? Are you at the bookstore right now?"

"Where are *you* right now?" he asked, skipping over my questions.

I named off the expressway, walking toward the road to find a mile-marker or other sign of identification.

"I'll come to you," he promised. "I had a cancellation, so I have some extra time."

"Whoa, thanks, Sean, but I'm surrounded by law enforcement right now," I interjected. "And I don't have a place to store the products, anyway, because my car is completely destroyed."

"We'll work something out," he assured me. "I don't like a fellow smuggler being in such a bad situation—all of those cops are going to be suspicious of you, and someone's obviously out to get you, so...I'll help you out."

"Thank you!"

"I'll be there as soon as I can." He hung up.

Chrystina and Jake were talking, so I didn't share with Jake right away that Sean was coming. When I walked up to the pair, they were discussing favorite flavors of ice cream, of all things. Chrystina laughed flirtatiously, messing with her hair again. *Oh, boy.*

The police wanted to ask Jake and me a few questions, apparently to make sure that we weren't purposely trying to endanger the lives of other drivers by setting our car on fire. Something about our tone of voice must have convinced them that we were too freaked out and surprised by the fire and subsequent explosion to have planned it ahead of time. Strangely, they did not ask us where we were headed; I don't know if Chrystina had already informed them of my answer or what, but I was grateful that I did not have to try to convince more people of the "buying a new book" story.

When Chrystina offered us a ride again, I told her that we had a friend coming to pick us up.

Jake looked at me strangely. "Really?"

"Yeah, my friend that called earlier offered to help us out when I told him what happened," I said carefully.

"Oh." Jake frowned.

"All right then, well, there will be people around here working on the clean-up for a while longer," Chrystina said, sounding disappointed that we had not chosen her for a ride. "I need to get back to work. You guys take care."

"Thanks," I told her.

"Yeah, thanks," Jake mumbled. When Chrystina had walked several yards away, he turned to me. "What's going on? Is somebody actually coming to get us? Wouldn't it just be better for us to ride with her, since she offered?" He sounded a little too eager to run after her and accept that ride.

"Sean's coming," I said. "He thinks someone purposely messed with my car."

"So are we going to rent a car now or what?"

"I think that's our only option."

Sean showed up fifteen minutes later, and we drove away from the scene, leaving our contact information with the police. Over the next couple of hours, we rented a red Concorde with a roomy trunk, and Sean followed us to a Wendy's a few miles away to transfer the load. I handed over the check, and he left quickly, needing to make it somewhere else in time for one of his appointments.

I was giddy over the successful smuggling session, and even Jake commented that it seemed as though I couldn't stop smiling.

"Everything just kept going wrong; I got to the point where I thought we were never going to get the products," I said.

Now on better terms, Jake and I decided to eat at an upscale Italian restaurant for lunch instead of getting fast food again. This time we might be able to comfortably make the conversation necessary for a sit-down meal.

The boxes were safely tucked in our trunk, and although I would need to purchase a car when I arrived home, the loose ends in mine and Jake's relationship were somewhat resolved and the business side of my life would be able to continue now that I had the herbal remedies necessary for my clients. What had started out as such a horrible road trip was turning out well, and I decided to let Jake drive for a while so that I could take a nap and continue on in my state of calm.

# # #

Police lights flashed one hundred feet behind us in the fog.

"What *now*? What do I do?" Jake whispered. "What do I *say*, Grace?" He shakily swerved over to the gravel, palming a small bottle of Intenzyme Forte resting in the ashtray and thrusting it under his seat before coming to a complete stop.

I couldn't answer him; I was grabbing frantically for a box resting by my feet. I dumped the box's contents onto the floor of the backseat and shoved my fingers into my hair to pull it taut before leaning forward and vomiting into the green bubble-wrap-lined cardboard depths. Stuffing myself full of lasagna, breadsticks, and cheesecake after having such a stressful day had been a mistake. Staring into the mess, I drew a shallow breath. "You cooperate and agree that you were speeding, Jake. He had no other reason to pull us over." I reached for a tissue from the paraphernalia on the floor and wiped my mouth before dropping it into the box. "I need some elderberry tea or something after he leaves."

A blonde policewoman who looked to be barely out of high school was the one who strode up to our candy apple red Concorde. As I watched her approach in the side mirror, I realized it was Chrystina. What on earth? I shifted the box out of my lap and down to the floor, cracking open my window to air out the sour smell swelling inside the vehicle.

"We meet again," she said in greeting. Chrystina seemed a little too pleased to see Jake. If she had pulled us over just so that she could talk to him again...I couldn't help but smile a little when her nose crinkled as a wave of stomach acid odor wafted out his window.

I rested my head against the back of the seat and closed my eyes while Jake talked to her. His cologne drifted in my direction as he shifted in his seat, and my throat spasmed in reaction.

"Are you all right, Grace?" Chrystina asked, genuine concern lacing her voice.

I looked over at her. She had bent down and was studying the box distastefully.

"Just the flu or something. Planning to get rid of that box at the next dumpster we come to," I explained.

She nodded sympathetically. "I'm not going to give you guys a ticket, since I know you're having a really bad day. But consider yourself warned. Watch your speed, Jake. Hope you guys have a good weekend."

Jake rolled up his window and turned to me gleefully. "How lucky is that?! Chrystina is pretty much the coolest cop ever."

I nodded, annoyed. "Can you reach those tea bags in the backseat?"

"Oh. Sure." He twisted to grab the soft-sided cooler on the floor in the back, lifting it into his lap and unzipping it.

A tap at the window caused us both to jump. Jake's head jerked up to face the unexpected sound, and I knew he probably had the look of a little boy caught with an extra cookie. Why had Chrystina returned?

"Jake…" I warned softly as he unrolled his window for the policewoman once more.

"Sorry to bother you again. I forgot to tell you that one of your brake lights is out."

"Ohhh…okay, thanks," Jake stuttered. His large hand was spread protectively over the bright yellow cooler and smashing its top down around the glass bottles of pills and box of tea inside. "It's a rental car, so it's not really our fault."

"I know. Here's just a friendly reminder." She smiled while handing him a slip of paper, and I noticed that her lips appeared shinier than when she had stood at his window the first time. "I won't bother y'all anymore. See ya."

"Bye, Chrys," Jake said.

I slid the cooler out from under his hand and flipped it open while he watched her retreat in his mirror. Grabbing a tea bag, I commented, "Jake, you'd better get moving. She might get suspicious if we keep sitting here." I opened a bottle of water and stuffed the thin bag of herbs into the opening. Elderberry tea tasted gross enough when it was hot, but I knew it would be especially nasty drinking it lukewarm like this. Oh, well, better than nothing. It should help my stomach.

"Whoops." He blushed, checked to see if the road was clear, and pulled out. "You want to stop at that Burger King to throw away your special box?" He pointed to the sign about half a mile down the road.

"That works for me."

Jake hummed sympathetically, turning into the Burger King parking lot and stopping by the dumpster. I carried my box over on shaky legs, hefting it in to join all the other revolting smells of rotten food. As I slid back into the car and shut the door, Jake gently pulled my arm toward him. "Push here," he said, applying pressure to my inner wrist with his thumb. "That's for nausea."

"Thanks," I replied, obeying. "Did she honestly write down a reminder for you to get your brake light fixed? I bet there's a phone number on that piece of paper." I snatched it from the cup holder where he had set it.

Jake blushed a second time. "I highly doubt it, Grace."

"Whatever." I smiled and read aloud, "'If you're interested, give me a call sometime: 543-6731.' Oh, for Pete's sake."

"Are you joking, or does it really say that?" Jake craned his neck over to my side of the car, and I tilted the paper so that he could verify it. "Sure enough. Hey, maybe this isn't such a bad day after all."

I rolled my eyes and changed the subject before his head became too large for his own good. "Are you awake enough? Do you want me to drive for a little bit?"

He looked at me skeptically. "Pretty sure that at this point I can't trust you not to retch all over the steering wheel. I think I'll be all right for a while longer."

"Thanks," I repeated, inwardly relieved that he didn't mind driving. "I owe you."

Eight hours later, Jake and I stood in my closed garage and opened the spacious trunk of the rented Concorde. Rows and rows of small boxes holding bottles of pills, small vials of homeopathic remedies, jars of salve and powders, plastic baggies filled with herbal tea bags, and many other illegal substances were nestled from the front to the back. "We made it," Jake said, relief visible on his stubbled face as he ran a hand through his dark, earlobe-length hair and yawned. "I'm going to go get some sleep now. Grace, I'm glad—I'm glad we were able to work things out."

"Me, too," I said. "I guess Candace knew what she was doing after all when she sent us on this trip. I don't know what would have happened if I'd gone by myself."

"Now that we're back, I think I actually enjoyed it," he commented. "I might want to go some other time if Candace ever backs out again."

"I'll keep that in mind," I replied. "Now go; get some rest."

# # #

I was up at 5:00, feeling much better and ready to assist my customers. The night before I had been too ill and exhausted to listen to the answering machine, but now I knew I could not put it off any longer. The past couple of days I had programmed my phone calls at the office to be forwarded to my home phone. Grabbing a pad of paper and a pen, I settled my mug of pepper-

mint tea onto a coaster and sat at my desk, feet propped on
a stack of three thick books about parasites. The answering
machine began spewing forth its litany of messages.

"Hi, Grace, this is Tonya Lynchwood. I was just
wondering if you have an appointment open tomorrow for
Trevor. He seems to be having some kind of a reaction to that
stuff you gave him last time…"

"Grace, this is Keisha. Just wondered if you wanted me
to come into work tomorrow—my friend is having surgery and
wants me to baby-sit if possible…"

"This is Jim Carlton. I would like to order some vitamins. Call me back…"

"Grace, I just wanted to tell you that these liver cleanses
are amazing! This morning I…"

Unfortunately, my appointment book was at the office,
so I would have to wait to find a spot for Trevor. My secretary
Keisha, on the other hand, would need to know right away if
she should come into work or not, so I called her. I had hired
Keisha on the basis that I only needed her a couple of times
each week, and I would always try to let her know as far ahead
as possible what days I would require her help. This week I had
purposely left open so that she would be unaware of the smuggling and consequently innocent if ever asked about it. All she
would know was that one day the cabinet was almost empty, and
the next time she came into work the supply was replenished.

I showered and ate a grapefruit with my usual three cups
of coffee (a bad habit I have tried many times to give up). I then
gathered up the notes I had taken from my phone messages and
left for work, driving carefully to protect my cargo.

My office was tucked in the back corner of a health food store named Organic Purity, which in turn was jammed between a Krispy Kreme and a Jo-Ann Fabrics. Health food stores were not illegal yet, as long as they were only selling food and not actual vitamins or other "medicinal" products. Organic Purity did carry vitamins, but they kept them out of sight from the customers and a customer had to provide an awful lot of information in order to be able to be trusted that he or she was not planning to use the vitamins as incriminating evidence against the store. They did not advertise anywhere that I had a bioenergetic practice there, but instead news of my business traveled by word-of-mouth. Up until Codex, I had had more clients than I had time for, but several of them cancelled as soon as the law went into effect, too scared to risk punishment. Although my clients would not get in as much trouble for coming to me as I would for dispensing to them, they were still in danger of fines and potentially jail time, depending on their level of involvement.

It was 6:30 in the morning, and since Organic Purity didn't open until 8, none of the employees were there yet. I had my own key, and so I let myself in, turning on a few lights and making sure the situation was secure before lugging everything out of my trunk and into my special cabinet in the back.

My office contained a small reception area just large enough for Keisha's desk, a copy machine, and two chairs for clients to wait in. The room in which I performed my testing was slightly larger, but it was still a bit more crowded than I would have liked. The owners of Organic Purity charged me incredibly cheap rent, though, so I stayed on. Before the law, when business was booming and I was saving a lot of money, I had been checking into other office spaces to rent—something in which my business was the forefront and not hidden behind another larger business. Unfortunately, that dream didn't seem like a possibility right now.

I flipped through the appointment book, looking for an opening for Trevor Lynchwood. The only available spot from now until next week was 10:30 a.m. today. I decided I'd better wait a few more minutes before I called since it was still so early. After leaving Jim Carlton's request on a Post-it for Keisha to deal with later, I spent the next hour ripping open boxes and alphabetizing products on the cabinet's shelves before a knock came on my door.

"Sarah! So great to see you again! It's been so long!" I enveloped my customer in a hug.

Sarah, a shy twenty-year-old, smiled and nudged her glasses higher on her nose. "It's good to see you, too, Grace."

"Come on in. Hi, I'm Grace," I said to the teen girl standing beside Sarah and the middle-aged man standing behind them both.

"Anna," the girl replied. She was sickly thin, and her face had a slight yellowish tint to it, but she smiled up at me hopefully. I assumed she had come to observe Sarah's appointment to see if it was something she would be interested in for herself.

The man, large dark circles under his eyes and graying hair ruffled up at the crown of his head, also smiled at me and shook my hand. "I'm Tom."

"Did you see the news this morning?" Sarah asked, dragging one of the chairs from reception into my already tight office space. I was confused by the fact that she didn't settle into the client chair closest to my computer, but I didn't address the issue right away. She had been here plenty of times to know where she should sit.

"No, I haven't turned on the TV yet today," I replied.

"The FBI arrested an acupuncturist last night in Portland. They have to hold the trial yet, but early estimates are that he could end up imprisoned for twenty years."

CHAPTER EIGHT

We discussed the situation in Portland for a few moments, most of the conversation occupied with Sarah telling me how brave I was for continuing my business despite all of the threats surrounding me. I assured her that instances such as the arrest of the acupuncturist, although frightening, were not enough to dissuade me. I was also trying to convince myself of this the whole time we were talking about it. Truthfully, Sarah's sharing about the acupuncturist shook me to the core, especially because I had a friend who was a bioenergetic practitioner out near Portland. That easily could have been me. Twenty years in jail.

Sarah tended to worry about stuff too much already, though, and she seemed even more anxious today. I made a mental note to test her for the Bach Flower remedies Mimulus and Aspen, which were both known for correcting the emotional imbalance of fear. The smuggling trip had been awful, and I was still going to have to deal with the consequences of my car exploding for seemingly no reason, but I finally felt as though I could help people again. That last week before the trip had been hard—I had continued with appointments, but very few of my clients had been able to take products home with them, and I hated to tell them everything that was wrong with their bodies and then not provide a solution to their problems.

"So, let's get started," I said. "Anna and Tom, are you here to watch today? Are you relatives of Sarah's?"

"Well, Sarah offered…" Tom's voice trailed off, and he looked at Sarah and then me questioningly, as though I should have already known what was going on.

"Grace, I meant to call and tell you about this, but I forgot. Would it be okay if Anna takes my appointment slot today? She's been having a lot of problems, and I know you're always so booked. Anna doesn't have a lot of time."

"Um, okay." This had caught me off guard, but it was fine. "Well, I can try to hurry, but no promises. It usually takes longer to test a new client than it does to test someone who's been here before."

"What Sarah means is…" Anna paused. "I don't have a lot of time in general. To live. Or so doctors have told me."

She said it so matter-of-factly. I wondered how someone so young could come to terms with her own mortality just like that.

"Anna, how old are you?" I asked quietly.

"Sixteen," she replied. "I was diagnosed with leukemia a few weeks ago. I guess it's in late stages of development, and my doctors haven't given me much hope. Sarah and I have gone to church together forever, and she told me about you after the service last week. I was hoping maybe you would be able to help me get better."

"Anna, I would love to help you get better," I said carefully. "Quite honestly, though, I don't have any experience helping people with leukemia. In the past, when clients have come to me with cancer, I've referred them to a cancer clinic on the East Coast where they offer alternative approaches instead of chemotherapy and surgery. Last I heard, that clinic had temporarily closed down after Codex was passed here, but I'd be more than happy to try to get in touch with my contact there and see if they're taking on new clients yet."

Anna looked like she was about to cry, and I had to clear my throat to keep my own tears away. I felt so bad for her; I wanted to help her, but I didn't know if I could. In my classes, they'd always taught us to pass serious cases like this on to specialists, *especially* when a minor was involved.

"But…I don't think…I don't think my mom will let me," Anna finally squeaked out. One tear spilled over and trailed down to the corner of her mouth. "My mom didn't want me to come today, but my dad and I thought it was worth a shot, so he said he would bring me."

Tom nodded reluctantly and ran a hand through his hair. "Grace, are you sure you can't help us? It was all I could do to get my wife to agree to bring Anna here today. The family's already under so much stress right now; I would prefer if we could keep this treatment as simple as possible. Anna's doctors have basically told us there's a ten percent chance of her living beyond the next few months. That tells me that if we're going to do something to fight the leukemia, we need to do it as soon as possible. Even if that clinic *is* taking clients right now and if I could convince my wife it's a good idea, it still might be a month before we'll be able to take Anna out there."

I sighed. If I helped her and something went wrong, her mom could turn me in. Her dad could even end up getting angry and turning me in, even though he was so agreeable to everything now. This was a really dangerous situation. "Let me call my contact at the clinic and see if they're taking anyone. Then we'll go from there. Hang on a few minutes, all right?"

I grabbed my cell phone out of a drawer and walked through reception and out into Organic Purity. As risky as it was for me to peruse the store while talking about illegal supplements, I didn't want Tom, Anna, and Sarah to listen in on my conversation.

No one was near the produce section, so I headed over there. Tara answered just as I was about to hang up. "Hey, Grace."

"Hey, I have a new client who has just come to me to help her with leukemia. I'm really not comfortable trying to tackle that issue. Are you guys back open yet at the clinic?" I said it in just barely more than a whisper, keeping an eye out for eavesdropping shoppers.

"Oh, Grace, you didn't hear? We're relocating to Mexico. We hope to have everything up and running in about three months."

"Oh." I was going to have to go back to Anna and tell her there was no one who could help her. This was far more stressful than the smuggling trip. "Do you—do you know of any alternative clinics that are still open in the States?"

"No. I'm sorry, but everything I know of has shut down."

"Okay." I thought for a few seconds. "I need your

opinion on something. Do you think it's a horrible idea for me to try to help this girl?"

"I think you're fully capable of helping her, but I would advise against it."

I ended the conversation and walked slowly back to my office. So, basically, anybody who came to me with cancer needed me to help them, or else they wouldn't have any help from anyone. *Uggghhhhh.*

Everyone looked up at me hopefully.

I cleared my throat. "The clinic is moving to Mexico and won't be open for three months. Anna and Tom, I need you guys to listen to me closely. Like I said earlier, I don't have any experience helping people get rid of cancer, but I have studied up on it and might be able to give you some products that will help. You need to know, though, that everything I'm going to tell you to do is going to be a lot of work. I've had several people come to me with other serious conditions who did not improve because they decided it wasn't worth all of the work. You're going to have to treat earning your health back as though it's a full-time job."

"I'll do *anything*," she promised. "I'm not afraid of dying, but I really don't think it's my time to go. I want to get better."

I smiled. "Okay." I grabbed a blank information form from Keisha's desk. "I need you to fill this out, and then we can get started."

The way my computer program illustrates the body's condition is through a picture of a circle, and then each part of the body that is unhealthy (or "unbalanced") is a small yellow point outside of the circle. One would think that someone who has a serious disease like leukemia would have more points outside of the circle than someone who has, say, just a sore throat. This is not the case, however. My program does not necessarily list "leukemia" as a diagnosis, either—it will show the organs of the body which are laden with toxins but will not always give the same name to the condition as a typical medical doctor would. In Anna's case, several of her organs were severely unbalanced, including the liver, spleen, gallbladder, and heart, but I had seen other clients with similar problems who had never been labeled by anyone as having leukemia and who had been able to clear up their issues by following my recommendations. I gave her a strict regimen to follow to boost her immune system and destroy the cancer and ended it all by repeating once again that I did not have experience with cancer clients but felt these things I told her about would improve her health.

"Thank you," Anna told me repeatedly. She seemed so excited and grateful to get started on it all.

As we walked out to the front desk to add up her bill and to get the products out of my cabinet for her, Keisha walked in, travel mug of tea in one hand and overloaded green purse in the other. Her face was flushed, and she seemed a little frazzled, ripping off her coat as soon as she had set everything down.

"Good morning, Keisha, how are you?" I asked, printing off Anna's bill and pulling bottles from the cabinet.

"Much better now that I have my coat off," she said, gripping at the neck hole of her shirt and flapping it back and forth. "I was so warm."

That would make sense since it had to be at least seventy degrees outside already today. "Why did you even wear a coat today?"

"I just bought it, and it's so cute," she gushed. "I couldn't wait any longer to wear it."

Nineteen years old, a part-time student at the local community college, Keisha was studying fashion merchandising and couldn't turn down style for comfort. She was a family friend, and when Keisha was looking for a job, my parents asked me if I knew of anywhere she could work. I went one better and offered her a job. At the time, my parents thought it was a great solution; now that my business was illegal, they tried to persuade me that I shouldn't let Keisha work for me anymore.

"She's just a kid," my mom said. "You don't want to wreck her life."

"Mom, she's an adult. She's only six years younger than I am. It's her choice; I need an assistant, so if she doesn't stay, I'm just going to have to find someone else to take her place. Either way, I'm going to have to rope someone into this with me." To be fair, I had talked to Keisha about the situation after my parents got on me about it. I had explained the possible consequences of her choice to continue working for me, and she said that she might change her mind later on, but for the time being she was comfortable with her job. Plus, I paid her $10.00 an hour, and most of her friends were only making $8.00—I think that was the largest factor in her decision, even though she gave me a big speech about how dedicated she was to the cause of bioenergetics.

"The test is $100," I said to Anna, "and then here is the total of all the supplements." I handed over the bill, wondering what price she'd been expecting and whether she or her dad would say, "You know what? I don't want to do this after all."

Tom and Anna didn't seem fazed by the price. Tom

whipped out a credit card and handed it over without protest.

Sarah was pulling something out of her own purse. "Anna, I want to pay for the test for you. I would pay for the whole thing if I could, but that's all I can afford to give right now."

Unexpected tears rose in my eyes. I knew Sarah didn't have a lot of money to work with—she was a college student and had an apartment and a car to pay for.

Anna started to protest while Tom stared in shock at Sarah, but Sarah held up her hand and started writing out a check for $100.

"Thank you," Anna whispered, and her tears went further than mine did, tracking down her yellowed face.

As I was pulling two products for Anna out of my cabinet, one of the owners of the health food store knocked on my door and came inside. I greeted her warmly but instantly felt ill at ease when she looked suspiciously at the pills in my hand. Sarah said hi to her, but then we just kept on talking while I finished ringing Anna up.

"Do you want to re-schedule your appointment, Sarah?" I asked. "I have some openings coming up in the next two or three weeks."

"Yeah, how about three weeks?" Sarah said, and we quickly agreed on a date and time.

"Have a good day, you guys," I said as we wrapped every-thing up. I gave Sarah and Anna each a hug and shook Tom's hand. "Anna, call me if you have any questions. You should probably come back in four weeks for a check-up and so that we can update your supplements, so let me know if you decide to continue with this treatment."

As soon as Anna and Sarah walked out, I smiled at the owner, Karly Smith. "Hey, how are you?"

"I'm well," she replied distractedly, still looking behind me at the cabinet. "Grace, what do you keep in there?" She pointed behind me.

I opened the doors to show her. "Just my supplements and homeopathics and vitamins and everything." I couldn't help but grin a little at how nice and neat everything looked inside.

She rubbed her forehead. "Grace, I'm sorry, but I can't have you keeping that stuff here."

"What do you mean?"

"It's too much of a liability." She bit down on her lower lip. "I'm sorry. You can continue your practice here, but only if you don't sell these products."

"I don't understand…" I wouldn't be a very good "doctor" if I couldn't give my clients their "medicine," now would I? "But you guys sell illegal vitamins and things—"

"Yes, but not nearly as many as you do. If you get caught, my store will be shut down. And I can't risk that."

"So…" I still didn't completely understand.

"So, these products need to be gone by the end of the day. I don't care where you take them, just get them out of my store. Quickly." I had never seen something bother Karly so much. Usually we got along well. "The health inspector is coming in tomorrow. He's going to be looking all over, and we don't want him to notice anything illegal."

That made sense. "So, I can move everything back in after tomorrow?"

"No."

"Okay…"

"And I've been meaning to let you know that I'm going to have to raise your rent by $200 a month. The store has not been bringing in as much profit lately, and I have to pay the bills somehow."

Two hundred dollars more per month?! I added that up in my head, also thinking of the number of clients I had lost in the past few weeks due to their fear of the government. "I don't think I can afford that, Karly."

She shrugged. "Well, let me know in the next couple of days."

And that was that. I couldn't help but think she had probably been hoping to run me off in the first place. I understood that I was a risk, but I thought that she and I stood for the same things. Apparently not. Now I was going to need to find a new office *and* a new car. I tried to remember what it was that I didn't like about journalism.

CHAPTER NINE

The following night I sat at my kitchen counter with a notebook and pen, evaluating my job and why I kept doing what I did. Seriously, knowing that I was no longer going to have office space at Organic Purity made me think that maybe I should return to journalism. Unless I became an overseas correspondent for a war or something, there were definitely fewer risks with journalism than there were for a bioenergetic practitioner. But when I wrote down all the perks of journalism versus bioenergetic practitioner, there weren't too many. Basically it came down to that I could either have a legal job that I hated or an illegal job that I loved. My parents called while I was in the middle of choosing.

"Sweetie, I came across this ad in the paper, and I couldn't wait to tell you about it." I could hear the crinkle of newspaper on my mom's end of the line. "Lowell Publishing is hiring a new editor! You would be so great for the job!"

"It does look like a good job, Honey," my dad added. I hated it when they tag-teamed me.

The thought of editor did sound better than the idea of staff writer for a local paper or magazine, though. My parents lived an hour and a half away from me, so I didn't receive the same paper that they did. "Will you mail me the ad?" I asked.

"Sure." My mom sounded pleased at my expressed interest. When my career became illegal, my parents both grew concerned and tried to convince me that maybe I should find some other way to make money. Up until now, I hadn't been very cooperative with their suggestions.

We talked a few more minutes; I didn't tell them that I was about to lose my office—I didn't want any more pressure from them about taking a writing job (a little bit of pressure was fine; too much made me desire a writing job even less).

When we had hung up, I stood and decided to walk around my house a bit to stretch while processing all of my thoughts. I ended up in the basement. The large, open floor was carpeted in dark blue, and one ancient recliner was resting in the corner farthest from the stairs. My parents had given it to me when I moved into this house—they had owned that chair for at least twenty-five years before it became mine. It wasn't in the greatest shape—the fabric was stained in a couple of places, and the texture was worn thin in a few spots, but it was still comfy. I tended to forget about it, though, because I hardly ever came down here. A smaller space meant to be a bedroom contained a few boxes of things I didn't need but couldn't bear to part with, like old college papers that I'd earned *As* on and favorite stuffed animals from when I was a kid. An unfinished bathroom painted in a horrid shade of rotten egg yellow took up another corner. Other than these things, there was nothing in the basement.

What if…? I looked around at the space with new eyes. If I re-painted the basement, beautified the bathroom, maybe divided up the large recreation area into two separate rooms, brought in a couple of desks…I could have my office in my basement. It seemed as though it would be a lot easier to keep my business under wraps if it was in my house as opposed to renting space somewhere else. I would have to try harder to keep the upstairs of my house clean, since everyone would have to go through part of that in order to get to the basement, but I was sure I could handle cleaning a little more frequently. Nothing would be ready to go for a few weeks while I fixed up my basement, but I should be able to be back up and running in a month or so.

My phone rang again, and I ran upstairs to grab it. A phone was another thing that I did not keep in the basement.

It was Candace.

"How's your grandpa?" I asked. I had tried to call Candace when Jake and I had gotten back from North Carolina but had only been able to leave a message.

"He's doing better," she said, sounding relieved. "He's out of the hospital now. I heard yours and Jake's trip was pretty interesting…"

I gave her a compact version of what had happened, figuring from what she'd said that she had already heard Jake's side of it. "Candace, I have to admit that I was pretty mad at you when I found out that Jake was coming with me," I said, half-teasing and half-serious. "But, as usual, you knew best. I'm really glad that Jake and I were able to work things out."

"Were you able to *really* work things out?" she asked, and

I could hear the smile in her voice.

I rolled my eyes. "Candace, we're just friends now. I don't think it'll ever be anything more than that."

"Okay, okay," she conceded. "Have you talked to Jake in the last couple of days?"

"No."

"He emailed me tonight and said that the chiropractor who he shares an office with is moving to Mexico to open up a practice there. In two weeks Jake won't have an office anymore."

"Whoa, really? That kind of happened to me yesterday." I explained Karly's reasoning to Candace, and she agreed that it sounded as though Karly had just been trying to find a semi-polite way to get rid of me. "I was worried about it, but I think I just decided that I'm going to open up my business in my basement. I've got all of this space I'm not using—it'll be perfect."

Candace was silent for a moment. "Grace…" she said hesitantly.

I was instantly suspicious. "Yes, Candace?"

"You and Jake could open up a business together in your basement! You could charge him rent for his office space, and that would help you pay your bills even if you can't get your client number up as high as it used to be. I bet you could even talk him into helping you finish off your basement."

"Candace, I know I said that Jake and I are friends now and that we worked everything out, but I don't know if we're close enough that we could work out of the same office—out of my *house*, for Pete's sake…" Yeah, I didn't foresee that one working well at all.

"Well, just think about it," she said defensively. "It's just an idea. I won't be offended if you choose not to do it."

"It's a decent idea, Candace, if the history between Jake and me were any different, but—I don't know. I'll give it some thought," I promised.

CHAPTER TEN

After calculating an approximate figure for how much it was going to cost to re-finish my basement and comparing it with how much money I made per week and how much I had saved up in my bank account, I decided that perhaps it would be beneficial to invite Jake to be my business partner. Even though things were better between us now, I still wasn't sure that it was a great idea to own a business together. But I was going to share mine and Candace's idea and leave it up to him to make the choice.

When I finally worked up the nerve to call and ask, I only got his voicemail. And when he called me back a couple of hours later, I missed his call. The message he left was sweet, though.

"Hey, Grace. Got your message. I don't know if I want to do the whole business partner thing or not, but while I'm deciding I'll help you finish off your basement, if you want. Let me know if and when you want me to come over and help."

I purchased the materials that I thought I would need and then invited a few friends and my parents to come over and help the next weekend, offering food in exchange for their services, along with the promise that I would do my best to make time in my schedule to assist them with their own upcoming home projects.

So at 9:00 Saturday morning, Jake, Keisha, my mom and dad, Candace, and two other friends of mine from college who lived nearby dropped in to work on my basement. Most of them could only stay a couple of hours, but Jake said he could stay all day if I needed the help. I took him up on that offer, not only because I needed to get my basement looking amazing as quickly as possible but also because I wanted another opportunity to see how well we would get along if we decided to go into business together.

At 3:00 we stopped for a snack break and sat outside on my deck while eating apples (I was impressed to see Jake actually eat something healthy after all the junk food he consumed while on our road trip. I guess he had been telling the truth when he said he didn't eat like that all the time.) A few leaves were just beginning to fade from emerald green into sweet corn yellow, and the bright sun reflected off of a large spider web suspended between two trees, a crispy brown leaf swaddled in the middle. A small wasp's nest under the corner of the wooden railing on the deck was buzzing as three wasps crawled around on the outside of it, creating a stronger fortress for their empire.

"So, I've been thinking," Jake said, picking at a suspicious spot on his apple with his thumbnail, "that it could work. I think we should try out a few more times of just 'hanging out' to make sure, but the business partner thing has the potential to be really great. We both need offices, and what's more out of the way and less conspicuous to the police than a home business? We're really taking a risk by doing anything other than a home-based business."

I nodded and threw my core into my big backyard so that the animals that frequently wandered through could nibble on it. I tried to throw it, anyway; the hour-glass-shaped object landed only about ten feet away from my deck. Jake laughed at my pitiful pitching skills. I just shrugged, knowing it was useless to even try to defend myself. I was terribly non-athletic. I had come to terms with it back in my late teen years, after trying out for my high school's basketball and volleyball teams and ending up with only a lot of muscle aches and no spot on either team.

"What do you suggest for 'hanging out' times?" I attempted to clarify his terms.

"You wanna go see a movie tomorrow?"

I glared at him, pursing my lips. "That sounds a lot like a date. This is never going to work if we just return to dating. I'm not interested, Jake, if that's what this is about. You blew it once—I'm not giving you another chance on that."

He looked at me sideways, eyebrows raised. "Well, what are your ideas for hanging out, then? Friends go see movies together. I was just suggesting a friendly type of activity. Probably anything I suggest could end up getting twisted into sounding like a date, even if I said, 'Grace, let's go blow our noses together.'"

I snorted. "Okay, okay, I see your point. Obviously, my basement isn't going to be completely remodeled by the end of today, so how about if we just stick with remodeling my basement for our 'hanging out' times for now, huh? That seems nice and neutral, and the sooner we get it done, the sooner we can both bring in money again, assuming that we both end up working out of my house."

"On one condition," Jake replied, holding up his pointer finger.

"What's that?"

"That you help me organize my closet."

I laughed. "Sure, Jake, sure. I'll go you one better. If you keep helping me work on my house, I'll give you two months' rent for free."

And so, just like that, we somehow agreed to be business partners without either one of us actually agreeing to be business partners.

# # #

I parked at the tiny café at the end of her street. I went in there last week to check the place out; the owners were in their seventies, model grandparent-types with thick glasses and hearing aids. Well, the man had hearing aids, anyway—the woman really needed to get some. It would take that couple hours to figure out that the extra car in their lot wasn't a customer's vehicle. They might never figure it out, in fact. It was the perfect base for my project.

I was feeling generous today, so I decided to give them some business and pick up some coffee to go.

"Have a cinnamon roll, Honey," the woman trilled at me after I paid for my coffee. She removed a gooey roll the size of a small watermelon from behind the fingerprint-spotted case and slid it into a white bag. "On the house." She grinned up at me through her huge plastic glasses, their gold chain swinging against her saggy neck and floral, polyester collar.

"Thank you, ma'am," I told her, taking the bulging bag from her. "I hope you have a nice day."

She didn't respond to me, a look of concentration on her face as she counted how many honeymooners were left in the case. Yes, she did indeed need hearing aids and was not very observant. Perfect.

# # #

The first few days that Jake and I worked on my basement, I told myself I didn't care that we were spending so much time together. I dressed in cruddy paint clothes that didn't match half of the time, showered but left my hair wet and pulled back in a ponytail or French braid, wore no makeup, and didn't even bother to put in my contacts a couple of the days, wearing my thick, outdated glasses instead. We started work early in the morning and ended late at night; I generally provided a meal or two for him each day but went to no extra effort to do so— it was always something easy, always healthy but not especially fantastic—typical things that I, as a single person, ate every day. We talked a lot but never about our past relationship. I did my best to keep from flirting, but a few times Jake's responses to my comments about various subjects left me wondering how he was interpreting what I said, and on several occasions (more frequently as the days passed), I was nearly positive that he was trying to flirt with me. Finally, I gave up on carefully evaluating everything I was going to say and just blurted out whatever came into my head first, the way I used to speak when we were a couple.

On the night before the sixth day of our basement team-work, I was lying in bed, thinking through some of the conversations Jake and I had had during the day and, before I could change my mind, I set my alarm for half an hour earlier than I had been getting up each day previously.

The next morning I used that extra thirty minutes to primp, all the while upset with myself for applying makeup and straightening my hair just to get dusty and sweaty during manual labor. I tried to convince my prying conscience that, as a very girly type of girl, I was tired of looking awful for so many days in a row and merely needed to be true to myself, but…that argument didn't work out well in the long run.

I was not disappointed when I opened the door to Jake at 8:00. He opened his mouth to greet me like usual but paused briefly once he actually took a look at me. I bit my lip so that I wouldn't smile too enthusiastically, and he quickly recovered, continuing his "good morning" with an appreciative grin.

In the workdays that followed, I continued to put in the extra effort to look nice and pushed down the voice nagging inside me that I probably shouldn't do anything to encourage a renewed relationship with Jake.

In three weeks the remodeling of my basement was completed, and it was finally Jake's and my first official week as business partners. After much deliberation, I had presented Jake with a key to my house. It was kind of an awkward thing to do, considering our past relationship. But I figured that if my house was going to be the base for our business, he really needed to be able to have access to his office whenever he wanted, and I didn't want to have to be tied to my house 24/7—hence, the key.

The night before opening, we decided to go out to dinner and a movie together. Jake paid for our dinner. I had been planning for us each to pay for our own, but I was secretly delighted that he did so.

"I realized too late that I didn't make sure it was fine with you if I scheduled appointments really early in the morning," Jake said as we waited for our server to return with his debit card. "I have one tomorrow at 7:30, but after tomorrow, if you don't want me to have people over to your house that early in the morning, I won't do it anymore."

"Oh, that's fine," I said, laughing. "My first appointment tomorrow is at 7."

"Perfect," Jake replied. "I guess our thoughts were along the same line, then." He didn't say what I was thinking—that an uncanny number of our thoughts had been along the same lines the past several days. I could tell that this thought occurred in his brain as well, though, when he reached for my hand and then thought better of it, awkwardly pulling his hand back and twisting his napkin instead.

I pretended not to notice.

CHAPTER ELEVEN

It was a drizzly morning. I accidentally chose to wear my tennis shoes with the mesh on the top and halfway through my walk found that my toes were soaked. Each tree I passed under plopped heavy raindrops onto the brim of my baseball cap, dull thuds on the otherwise quiet morning. Water ran in tiny trails off my raincoat, giving up when it was unable to permeate the plastic surface. The sun had yet to rise, and several of the streetlights were burnt out. Everyone else on the street was still in bed, including the dogs that usually barked at me. This was the earliest I had taken my walk, and it appeared to have been a good decision. The barking usually brought me close to screaming out in frustration. I craved quiet. It allowed me to think more clearly.

I walked past her house. Through the blinds, I could see that the kitchen light was on, and I mentally gave her props for getting up so early. The blinds started to crack open, and I slowed, watching carefully. The rain-drenched sidewalk suddenly seemed extra-squishy, and I looked down. I had stepped in a pile of dog crap.

# # #

"They're out there," Jake commented as he walked into my house around seven Thursday morning, two days after our special dinner and movie.

"Who's out there?" I drained my third cup of coffee and eyed the small amount remaining in the bottom of the pot. "Do you want some coffee?"

He shook his head. "I reserve coffee for special days. Days that I'm pretty sure I can't stay awake through without drinking some of that junk. I don't know how you stand it, Grace. Not only does it taste awful, you know how bad it is for you."

"Thanks for reminding me of what a hypocrite I am." I rolled my eyes. "I repeat, who's out there?" *No takers? All right, I'll finish off the coffee, thank you very much.*

"The cops." Jake hung his jacket on my oak coat tree.

I swallowed wrong and felt warm coffee in the back of my nose. "In my *driveway?*" I had assumed all along that hosting my clients at my house would be much more under the radar than renting space from the health food store or another location. Maybe I had been wrong; maybe I should have rented a legitimate office building.

"No. I passed one of them on your street, though. The car drove past your driveway a second time as I was getting out of my car."

"Do you think we should postpone our morning appointments, just to be safe?" I asked.

"What time is your first one?"

"I have a late start today because of a cancellation, so 8:00."

"My first one's at 7:30," Jake replied. "Let's play it by ear. We'll each keep our first appointment, and if the police continue to hang around, we'll cancel the rest."

"All right. Sounds good to me."

As I straightened the comforter on my bed and opened my blinds just a crack, I looked as far down the street both ways as my window would allow. My neighbor across the street, Kurt Doozenbury, was just opening his garage door and backing his white Corvette down the driveway for work. He always drove with the top down as long as there was no rain or snow to mess up his delicate hair transplants. His huge, precious house that he lived in with his nineteen-year-old wife was worth at least $200,000 more than any other house on the block. Really, he was the best possible person to have living across from me because he would never turn me in. Despite having a wife young enough to be his daughter, he was constantly on the prowl for new women and flirted with me every chance he got. Plus, there was a rumor that Kurt had been convicted of tax evasion in the past, which made me happy that he, too, was a law-breaker (although not in an honorable way) and decreased my concern that he would turn me in just to get some weight off his conscience.

As Kurt paused in his driveway before backing out into the street, a police car passed slowly, two officers sipping coffee in the front seat. Right behind them was a silver SUV, which pulled into my driveway. It had to be Jake's 7:30. The thirty-something female driver climbed out of her vehicle, adjusting her sunglasses while spying on the Carson Township Police car inching down the asphalt. She strode up to my front door carefully and knocked. I heard Jake walk to the entryway and let her in.

# # #

An abrupt, impatient pounding on my front door startled me from a late afternoon nap. Jake and I had decided it was best to cancel the majority of our appointments for the day since the police kept driving by. Jake went home at eleven, and I spent a few hours cleaning my house to a nineties dance CD that ended up serving as the only thing close to a workout that I'd participated in for about a month.

The scent of the cleaning products started to make me feel nauseous, so I'd chosen to lie down for a while. Ever since I had experienced that horrendous stomach illness during the smuggling trip, my digestion and overall sense of good health had continued to be screwed up. I had been so preoccupied with the start of Jake's and my business, though, that I hadn't made any decent attempts to correct whatever was wrong with me.

I peeked out the corner of my blinds and freaked at the sight of a cop car in my driveway. It had been one thing to be nervous earlier while they kept driving past, but I had mostly reassured myself and Jake that everything was going to be okay. Now my doubts returned, jagged edges poking at my previously calm, settled self.

I smoothed my hair with both hands and slid a finger

under each eye to clear away any smeared eyeliner and mascara from the nap. The front door seemed like a portal into a new world—a world in which I, in a twisted Jekyll-and-Hyde sort of way, was revealed to be a criminal instead of the respected healer that I had fought to become. I felt as though I were moving in slow motion, savoring the last few moments of the clean air in my own home before being pulled into the stale air of a federal prison. The darts of light showing through the small, square windows at the top of my front door pierced through crumbs of dust which I walked into slowly and suddenly imagined sucking into my lungs. This thought triggered a fit of coughing that possessed no genuine cause, and I paused to collect myself.

Another knock.

I kicked a pair of shoes aside and opened the door.

"Ms. Hampton?" One man and one woman stood on my tiny front porch. The woman looked a little familiar.

I tilted my head and tried to figure out where I may have seen her before. "Yes?"

"Do you know a woman named Suzanne Laird?"

"Yes, I'm acquainted with Suzanne Laird. Why?"

"We can't reveal too many details at this time, ma'am." The man pulled a notebook out of a pocket. "What is your relationship with her?"

"We're friends, but I don't see her that often."

"When did you last see her or speak with her?"

"About a month ago." At her last appointment with me.

"We have reason to believe that she's involved in a serious crime. Is there anything you can tell us that would point to her current whereabouts?"

I shook my head.

The woman, who had not spoken until now yet had also been staring at me as though she knew me from somewhere, handed over a business card. "We ask that you would please call us immediately if the suspect tries to contact you. And please remember that purposely withholding information that could help to solve a crime will incriminate you as well."

I nodded and accepted the card. "All right."

The pair turned around and headed to their squad car.

Confused, I shut and locked my door before taking a seat on the couch in my living room. So…was the crime they were referring to related to Suzanne's possession of natural remedies? Or something completely different? And who would have tipped them off to ask *me* questions about the situation?

Suddenly I knew where I had seen the policewoman before.

She was the one who had assisted Jake and me through the car explosion and then pulled us over and left him her number on the "friendly reminder" to get his brake lights checked. If she was local law enforcement in North Carolina, though, what was she doing in my neighborhood in Michigan?

CHAPTER TWELVE

Later that day, my mom called. I asked if I could call her back (I was in the middle of organizing hundreds of emails that I had been neglecting and didn't want to lose my rhythm); normally my parents are very agreeable to that sort of thing, but today my mom was quite forceful in her "No."

"What's going on?" I asked, minimizing my email so I could give her my full attention.

"We ate lunch with Grandma and Grandpa today, and they shared that Grandpa's test results came back yesterday."

I vaguely remembered that he had gone to the hospital for a few tests after a lingering illness. I hadn't paid that much attention. I love my grandparents and care about them, but I've never spent much time with them. Besides, they're close to eighty, and elderly people are bound to take longer to get over sickness than a typical person my age would. I hadn't even offered to test him on my computer, knowing that he would politely refuse.

"Grace, he has pancreatic cancer. Stage three." My mom's

voice caught, and I heard her sniff.

"What?" A diagnosis of pancreatic cancer is pretty much a death sentence in the traditional medical community.

"The doctors think it might be genetic; they highly recommended that everyone in the family get tested." She was full-out crying now. This particular grandfather was my dad's dad, but my mom, whose own father died when she was fourteen, has a very close relationship with my grandpa. "Your uncle's already scheduled a screening for Tuesday, and your dad's thinking about getting tested. They haven't been able to get in touch with Aunt Kate and Aunt Toni yet, but I'm sure they'll end up deciding in favor of the test as well." She paused. "Honey, I know you don't go to doctors, but, you know, it might be wise for you to get tested. It certainly wouldn't hurt anything…"

"Mom, if anything's wrong with me, it would show up on my own testing system," I argued. In the back of my mind I wondered how long it had been since I had tested myself or scheduled an appointment with Candace to test me. It had to have been close to a year. Although I wasn't concerned about pancreatic cancer for myself, it was in my best interest to get tested soon, just as a check-up for my body in general.

My mother sighed. "Okay, Honey. I love you. I'll do my best to keep you updated. I'm sure Grandpa would love to see you if you have time to drop in on him and Grandma."

"Yeah, I'll plan to do that soon," I said. Maybe this weekend. Now that my days wouldn't be so filled with home construction projects, I should definitely have time to visit my sick grandfather.

# # #

There were too many cops. I spent a large chunk of the day in the bakery, reading a novel and talking with the elderly couple. I wanted to walk by her house, but it didn't seem like the right time. Maybe later that night. I took a look at my map and marked out a route for another house I needed to check on. That was the problem—the supplies never lasted very long. I always had to be looking ahead, planning out the next location. Once again, the brief thought occurred to me that maybe my group and I should check into a better way to obtain our products, but Jim had so many reasons why this was a good idea that it was hard to argue with him. I really did feel bad this time—she and I had gotten close, and I didn't want to hurt her. Unfortunately, I had to do it anyway. It was all for the greater good.

# # #

Anna returned with her dad for another appointment the following day. She had clearly lost more weight in the last few weeks and even the whites of her eyes were beginning to look yellow to match her skin tone. I greeted her cautiously, uncertain as to whether I was about to receive an onslaught of complaints. Anna's control of her emotions far surpassed that of the majority of people three times her age, however. She smiled at me warmly, gently returning the hug that I offered. She held up a plastic Meijer bag, containing what I assumed from the shapes poking out were supplements and books.

"Grace, I have so many things to tell you!" she squealed. "Will you test me? Will you see if I'm any better?" At the end of that question, Anna suddenly gave the loudest, most awful smoker's type of cough I had ever heard, and it took her close to a minute to recover from it. I stood nearby, poised to help her if need be.

Finally, when her coughing fit had died down some, I asked if she would like a glass of water. She shook her head, unearthing a water bottle from the Meijer bag and taking a long drag. "Okay," she said, hoarse but somehow still incredibly enthusiastic. "Where's your new office?"

I smiled and led her downstairs. Tom trailed behind, even more quiet than the first time I had tested Anna. Once we were seated, I invited her to tell me what had been going on with her health since I had seen her last.

"Well, I think I'm feeling a little worse," she said, still with a smile on her face. "But all of these books of yours I've been reading act like that's a normal thing, like it means I have to feel worse before I can feel better, so I don't really mind feeling worse temporarily. I'm doing home school now instead of public school, so the times I don't feel the best don't equal missed school days. My dad has been helping out a lot; he's made a schedule for me each day of what times to take things and reminds me if I forget." She paused and directed a grin at her dad. "I have a doctor appointment coming up again at the end of this week. They keep pressuring me to do chemo, but I don't want to. Every once in a while I have a day where I feel so weak I can barely move, and I can only imagine that chemo would make me feel even worse, with fewer good results in the end."

"How is your mom responding to all of this?"

"She…" This was the first time today that Anna had looked discouraged. "She's really upset about it and thinks I'm making a huge mistake."

I nodded, absorbing all of this information. I knew all of the textbook answers to tell her what to do, and I had read plenty of stories of people for whom alternative means had been successful in solving their serious medical conditions, but my own body had never needed to fight off leukemia before, and none of my other clients had, either. After a few more minutes of talking, I pulled up Anna's file on my computer and re-tested her. She did, in fact, test worse; however, like she had said, that information agreed with what I, too, had read—during the healing process, a person tended to get worse as toxins were released into the system to be disposed of.

I suggested more supplements she could take to boost her immune system as it fought harder than it had ever needed to previously and recommended that she continue doing what she had been doing. At the end of the appointment, Anna slipped away to use the bathroom. Tom spoke as soon as she was out of earshot.

"Grace, I truly believe you're helping my daughter, but if she doesn't show some improvement soon, we're going to have to quit your program. My marriage has turned into a nightmare—my wife, Rachel, quit speaking to me weeks ago. She barely even talks to Anna anymore, except to make her feel guilty for trying your products. She yelled at Anna for fifteen minutes today before we drove over here."

There wasn't much I could say. I had no idea how long it might take for Anna to feel better. "I can't make any promises, Tom. I do firmly believe that Anna can get better, but as I said before, I have no experience working with cancer patients, so…I don't have a time frame in mind for you. You need to do whatever you feel is right for Anna and your family."

# # #

At noon Keisha, Jake, and I ate lunch together. I didn't usually prepare meals for all of us—normally we each went our separate ways for lunch hour or sometimes one or both of them packed a lunch and ate with me while I scrounged through my cupboards and ate an exciting lunch such as rice cakes with cashew butter or tuna on tapioca bread. Today, however, I had told them ahead of time that I would cook for them—sort of a celebration of our new business together. Keisha, always on the lookout for her next boyfriend, readily welcomed any extra time that she was able to spend with Jake. Although I still found myself interested in Jake as more than a business partner and friend, I did not feel envious of Keisha's obvious attempts to win his affection. I liked to think that I was much more mature and, due to our history together, if Jake and I were meant to be, no one could get in our way. Besides, Jake never seemed interested in Keisha, anyway. He was nice to her and even paid her extra to assist him with some office work, but he always seemed kind of oblivious to her flirting (or maybe was just trying to be polite).

I had worked hard on this meal, preparing homemade marinara sauce with hand-rolled meatballs for spaghetti, a large garden salad, homemade garlic bread, and strawberries with thick, homemade whipped cream for dessert. Keisha situated herself so that she sat in the chair right beside Jake, and I sat across from the two of them. While we were eating, Jake received a phone call on his cell and stepped away from the table for quite some time to talk. He returned as Keisha and I were just starting in on dessert.

"Sorry about that, ladies. This meal is delicious, Grace," he commented, digging in with renewed gusto and helping himself to another piece of bread.

"Is everything okay? You were gone a long time," I said.

"Oh, yeah, everything's fine. A, uh, friend is in town and we were just making plans," he replied vaguely, shoving a meatball into his mouth and looking everywhere but into my eyes.

I nodded as if I understood. *Plans for a date, perhaps?* I told myself I didn't care. Keisha didn't seem to care that Jake appeared to be withholding information; she was just glad that he was back. "Would you like some more water, Jake?" she asked sweetly.

He glanced at his glass. "I think I'm fine, Keisha, thanks."

She looked immensely disappointed.

Jake and Keisha both offered to help me clean up, but I refused, just grateful that our new business venture was going well and that the two of them were, overall, great people with whom to work. Keisha ended up going out to her car to text her friend or something like that, and I was in the kitchen alone, scrubbing dishes, when Jake walked up behind me, reached over, and splashed water up at me. I jumped back and turned, swiping him with my sudsy hand. He caught my hand before I could hit him, smiling at me mock-wickedly. I narrowed my eyes and managed to get him with my other hand, although he did grab that wrist after I hit him and began to tug me toward himself. I resisted, wanting to end up in his arms and yet knowing this was only going to complicate matters more.

Our lips had just touched when we both heard the front door swing open, announcing Keisha's return, and we pulled apart before she could round the corner and find us.

CHAPTER THIRTEEN

Over the next couple of days, I developed what soon became the worst cold I had ever contracted. I had to cancel my appointments and stayed in my room all day, trying to keep from spreading my germs to Jake's clients. I forced down as much elderberry tea, orange juice, and water as I could possibly fit in my stomach and even resorted to sucking on a piece of garlic (one of my least favorite remedies) in order to help my throat feel better and to strengthen my voice. For twenty-four hours straight, I could not talk in anything above a whisper. Instead of just having Keisha make business calls for me, I also used her to make a couple of personal calls, simply because I knew that the person on the other end of the line probably wouldn't be able to understand me. I went through two large boxes of Kleenex, and Jake was kind enough to give me a gift of a three-pack of Kleenex boxes when he arrived at work on day four of my illness.

This cold combined with the stomach flu at the end of the smuggling trip a few weeks ago added up to more sickness than I had experienced in the last three years. I decided that my immune system must be extra-compromised due to so much stress lately and vowed that I needed to put more emphasis on eating healthy. Maybe I would even need to give up my coffee addiction. I couldn't afford to have so many lost work days.

My health had improved some by the weekend, and I was excited to receive a package that I had special-ordered for Anna. It was getting more and more difficult for people to agree to send natural products in the mail since Codex went into effect, but this product had come from Mexico, where all kinds of healing methods were still practiced freely. I was convinced that this was something that was really going to help her, and I wanted to get it to her as soon as possible. Anna, however, lived about forty-five minutes away from me, making it a lengthy journey for either of us to just pick up and go. When I called to tell her that the item had come in, Anna suggested a meeting place—apparently, the church she had spoken of at her first visit was only fifteen minutes away from my house. With anyone else, I would have said that the idea had been suggested slyly, but Anna seemed to have too much goodness in her to be sly about anything. She didn't even try to convince me to actually come to the service. She simply said, "I'll be fifteen minutes away from your house on Sunday for church. Would you be able to meet me a few minutes before the service starts?"

I hadn't been in a church since I was twelve and wanted to say no, but I also really wanted Anna to get better. My desire to help her outweighed my lack of a desire to attend church. "I'll be there."

# # #

As much as I told myself that I wasn't going to be pulled into staying for the morning service—I was merely going to drop off the goods and go—I still found myself dressing up to meet with Anna, as though I were going to stay. I was so confused. Lately I had sent up a couple of random prayers for my grandpa's health, which was odd, because I couldn't remember the last time I had prayed for anything. Each time I did it, it caught me off guard. I would be in the middle of the prayer, and then, poof, realize, *Hey, I'm praying.* And then I would finish the sentence in my thought pattern and stop. It wasn't that I didn't believe in God, because I totally did, but more that I didn't think He was really that active on earth. So why bother praying? He's not going to do anything, anyway. It's a waste of time. In this particular case, I think the reason I was doing it was because there was nothing I personally could do for my grandpa. I knew he wasn't going to agree to accept my form of treatment, and there was not much modern medicine could do to help him. So, somehow, subconsciously, I had turned to God.

Weird.

Arriving at the church, I was crazy nervous. I quickly crinkled the side of my skirt in my hand as the wind sprinted up behind me with the force of an air horn, threatening to blow not only the hair off my head but also the clothes off my body. Two old, blue bulletins dating back to the nineties escaped from my small, monogrammed Bible, flattening themselves against the building before chasing each other around the corner. So much for making a good impression on the members of this church.

I would walk inside looking like a homeless person and feeling guilty for littering on their property.

An elderly gentleman in a suit fifteen feet ahead took pity on my bedraggled self and held the front door open. "Welcome to Charleston Community Church," he said. "Have you come here before?"

"No, actually, this is my first time," I replied, shaking his hand.

"Well, glad to have you," he said and provided directions to the sanctuary.

I looked around in the hall for Anna but didn't see her, so I moved into the auditorium. Clusters of people dotted the pews, chatting, rustling through bulletins, and reading about upcoming church activities on the PowerPoint presentation flashing in front. Padded with burgundy fabric, each row of pews could fit about ten people. There were three sections of pews spread out over the church, and I guessed that probably five or six hundred people could sit comfortably in the room. A large wooden cross dominated the back wall, and white rope lights glittered from the perimeter of the stage. I laughed out loud at the revolving disco ball dangling from the ceiling up front, casting pockets of light onto church members of all ages and reflecting in odd colors off of the small panes of stained glass lining the two side walls. A boy of twelve or thirteen walked up and down the aisles with a basket of Bibles, asking if anyone needed to borrow one for the duration of the service. Despite the casual atmosphere, I appreciated the fact that I did not feel overdressed in my skirt and three-inch heels: about half of the congregation was dressed in a similar manner, while the rest wore jeans (I even saw pairs of sweatpants on the couple standing four rows ahead of me). One thing was for sure: this church was much different than the legalistic one I had attended as a child.

I decided to take a seat and let Anna find me. I wasn't really sure what to do while waiting, though, so I fiddled in my purse, first pulling out some lip gloss and applying it, and then double-checking that my phone was set on silent, and then sorting through a collection of receipts.

"Hi, I don't think I've met you before," someone said.

I glanced up. A woman approximately my age was standing beside me, hand stuck out to shake with mine. The gold and brown tones of her clothing complemented her shoulder-length red hair.

"I'm Valerie."

"I'm Grace. Nice to meet you. Have you attended here for a long time?"

"Four years. I was here when David started the church." She pointed to a man sitting on the front steps of the stage, talking to a group of small boys who were showing him their new action figures. "He's the senior pastor."

Pastor David's broad shoulders were enhanced by the black suit coat stretched across them. His jeans and leather flip-flops made him look approachable and earthy, while his short, dark hair with a slight curl on the ends contributed to a look younger than the early to mid-thirty range I guessed him to be. When he smiled at something one of the boys had said, I smiled, too. David's grin was so genuine and relaxed that I somehow felt at home (and he wasn't even directing his happy face at me!). He seemed like the type of person you could trust with anything.

My evaluation of the pastor was interrupted by the sound of a familiar, cheerful voice. "Grace! You found it okay."

Although I was grateful that Valerie had come up to make me feel welcome, it was far more reassuring to see someone who I actually knew. Somehow, when I had heard Anna's happy voice, I expected to turn around and find her physical appearance to be healthier than when I had seen her last, but instead, she looked still worse. I don't know why I had anticipated improvement—after all, I had read more stories of cleansing than I could count, and there was rarely one which involved the person getting better right from the get-go. I suppose I was just worried that if Anna didn't feel at least slightly better soon, she and her dad would give up and quit.

I smiled and held up the full brown paper bag I had brought for her. "Here you go."

She looked pleased to see me dressed up and sitting in a pew. "Grace, I'm so sorry to do this to you—normally, of course, I would stay and sit with you, but I'm not planning to stay for the service. It's been a rough morning. I made it through Sunday school, and I think that's all I can do today. Sarah's not here this morning, either. She's on vacation with her family."

"Oh, I completely understand," I replied, meanwhile panicking that I was going to have to sit by myself. Maybe Valerie would offer for me to sit with her. As I glanced over to Anna's right, though, I noticed that Valerie had drifted off somewhere else now that I had another person to talk to. Perhaps I would just wait for Anna to leave and then I'd slip out, and she would never have to know that I hadn't stayed.

The longer I waited for Anna to leave the church,

though—person after person kept stopping her to talk—the more I realized that there was no way to get out of this situation gracefully. A screen in front had begun counting down five minutes until the service started, and Anna appeared to be in a deep conversation with someone in the back of the sanctuary. When there was just forty-five seconds left on the countdown, I saw Anna finally leave. By then, it was too late for me, and I felt myself beginning to sweat a little and have a reaction similar to what one might experience when claustrophobic. I wasn't sure exactly what about church made me feel this way, but the idea of sitting through the service all by myself was incredibly unsettling. I looked around frantically for Valerie but could not locate her. I pulled my purse, which was on the seat next to me, closer, so that it was leaning against my hip, and that made me feel slightly more secure, almost as if another person were sitting with me.

"I want to welcome everyone to Charleston Community Church and thank each of you who decided to risk trying us out." Pastor David's voice booming out from the stage and the reappearance of his smile made my heart dance. "If you need help finding something or have a question about the church or our beliefs, just stop one of the men or women sitting in these first few rows. They're our deacons, deacons' wives, office staff, trustees, etcetera. One of them should be able to answer any question you have, and of course, feel free to come talk to me, too. I would love to meet you, especially if this is your first time here." His eyes scanned the crowd, and I watched as his gaze paused a few different times; one of those times was on me. He brought his hands together, signaling an end to his opening speech. "All right, let's get this party started."

The band's volume increased suddenly, and Pastor David stepped off the stage as another man separated himself from the rest of the band and began to lead the congregation in the first song. I rose to my feet with everyone else and, surprisingly, thoroughly enjoyed the next hour and twenty minutes of singing and the sermon. Judging from the widespread collection of characters the church seemed to attract, I guessed that they might accept me, even if I told them about my job. In the row across from me, a man and a woman sat together, bundled up in layers of mismatched clothes. Every once in a while, when they shifted in their pew, body odor drifted over to me, and I discretely turned my head the other direction to gather in a fresh breath. The man, who was sitting on the end of the pew closest to me, had set a half-full black trash bag by his feet when he walked into the service. When we stood up for the closing song, his foot bumped the bag, and its wide, floppy mouth fell open in my direction, loose lips revealing a crooked, toothy cave of pop cans, ready to be cashed in for ten cents apiece.

A few rows behind that couple sat three guys and one girl who looked around seventeen, their faces studded with jewelry and tattoos lining the necks of two of the guys. The girl held a baby wrapped in a black fleece blanket with skulls decorating it. At the end of the service, I eavesdropped as a business-suit-clad woman near my mom's age went up to the foursome and inquired about the baby, whose name was apparently Zirconia.

There were probably fifteen teenagers and twenty-somethings with wildly-colored hair scattered throughout the church. One of the girls with lime green hair shook my hand and introduced herself and her boyfriend to me. "I'm a tattoo artist," she stated when I asked about her life. She grinned. "I offer fifteen percent off to people who attend this church. Not too many people take me up on it, though."

On my way out of the sanctuary, I heard someone jog up behind me. "Hey!"

I turned around. It was Pastor David. He stuck out his hand, and I returned his handshake. "I always try to talk to our first-timers one-on-one, and I wanted to make sure I caught you before you left forever." He smiled. "I'm David Michaels, by the way, except I'm guessing you probably already knew that."

"I'm Grace. I really enjoyed your sermon." I nervously ran a hand through my hair.

"Oh, thanks." He looked embarrassed, as if maybe he thought that I thought he had been fishing for a compliment. "So, do you currently attend church anywhere?"

"Uh…no. No, I don't." I really wished that I could tell this guy yes. It would have made me look like a better person, the type of person David might like…

If he thought less of me because of the no-church factor, though, his facial expression certainly did not reveal so. "Well, I hope you'll try us out again next week."

How could I say no to those incredible brown eyes and the most perfect smile I had ever seen? "Yes, I'm planning to come back."

CHAPTER FOURTEEN

Today might be the day. I had my car stocked with bags so that I would be fully prepared to complete my task at the first opportunity. I had also walked around her house a couple of times last night after she went to bed, contemplating the best option for entry. She was home for now, but it was a nice day, and it was Friday, which meant that her chances of leaving home for a few hours were higher than on a normal weekday. Maybe she and that chiropractor who shared her office would go out; they would make an attractive couple. If today didn't work out, I would have to make my move soon. Time was running out.

# # #

When late Friday afternoon arrived and my last client had left for the day, I realized that all I really wanted to do was get out of the house. The cops were still lurking around occasionally—why, I wasn't sure, since Suzanne didn't live anywhere near here, and I still hadn't seen her since her last appointment—and I just wanted to get away from the stress of it all. Once I knew that Jake's last patient had left and Keisha had gathered up her things and cleared out, I walked into his office to talk to him. We hadn't had any time alone together since the kiss in my kitchen, and I still wasn't sure where I wanted that to go.

Jake was working intently on some forms at his desk and barely glanced up when I entered the room. "Hey, Grace."

"Hey." I leaned against the doorjamb, thinking how I should phrase the question I was about to ask. I wanted someone to hang out with tonight, and Jake would be the easiest answer to that problem. I didn't want it to be a date (at least I was pretty sure I didn't want it to be a date), and, anyway, I was mostly opposed to women asking men out. I simply wanted to hang out as friends. "I was just wondering if you're up for a movie or something tonight." I held my breath, unsure how he would interpret this suggestion.

He finally gave me his attention. "Oh, that sounds fun, and I totally would be, but I already have plans. Sorry, Grace. Maybe next Friday?"

"Oh…sure, that's fine. Have fun tonight." I hung around a few more seconds, hoping he would elaborate on his plans, but he said nothing, merely continuing his work. I nodded, which he didn't see, and eventually turned around to head back upstairs and figure out someone else I could get together with tonight. My carpet was looking gross; maybe I should just stay home and clean.

"Grace?" Jake's voice called.

I stopped and turned around but didn't walk back into his office. "Yeah, Jake?"

"I meant to tell you earlier that I really like that shirt you're wearing today. The color makes your eyes sparkle."

I cocked my head to the side, smiled a little, and answered, "Thanks." *I cannot figure this man out.*

I decided to call Candace. I would have to drive farther in order to hang out with her, but it would be worth it—the two of us always had a good time together, no matter what. When she picked up the phone, though, she sounded stressed and out of breath.

"Candace? Is everything okay?"

"Yeah, I am just so behind on everything. My parents are visiting tomorrow, and my house is a disaster, and I have to go to this stupid housewarming party tonight for this couple I barely even know, and one of my clients got really mad at me today because I couldn't change her appointment to 10:00 instead of 9:00. I don't know, it's been kind of a rough day. What's up with you?"

"Oh, I was just checking if you wanted to hang out tonight. But I guess you already have plans, huh?"

"Unfortunately, yes." Candace sighed. "My dentist recently bought a new house and is having this huge party so that everyone can see it. I don't even know her very well, and I don't know her husband at all. I think she's just inviting everyone she knows in the hope that we'll give her fantastic gifts."

I tried to figure out who else I could call. My business had occupied so much of my time lately that I hadn't kept in close contact with any of my other friends. Most of them were married now, anyway, and consequently it was much more difficult to catch them for a night out. Maybe…Keisha? I couldn't figure out if that would be awkward or not. We'd never hung out before outside of work, but her parents had been friends with my parents forever, and she seemed like a fun girl, although she was a little too obsessed with dating. I tried to call her, but her phone went straight to voicemail, and I didn't want to put my night on hold waiting around for her to call back. So I hung up.

Maybe I would go grocery shopping instead. That way I could still get out of the house and get something important accomplished at the same time. I compiled a list, which ended up being rather long, and was inspecting my cupboards and refrigerator one last time trying to figure out if I should write anything else down when Jake told me goodbye and left for the day. There was no reason for me to stick around any longer, so I gathered up my purse and jacket and drove to Meijer.

I was selecting some organic grapes when I happened to notice the man picking out oranges from the display of citrus fruit several feet in front of me. He mostly had his back to me, but I could see enough of his face (and his flip-flops) to know that it was Pastor David. My breathing quickened a little, and I carefully set the bag of purple grapes in my cart, smoothing out my hair and brushing some lint off my shirt. Should I make my way over there and say hi or wait for him to spot me? He probably wouldn't even remember me, and then I would feel like an idiot if I said something to him. Perhaps I could just move so that I was in his field of vision more, and then if he felt like saying something, he could. I figured I was setting myself up for disappointment but couldn't stop from pushing my cart over to the other side of the display that he was standing at. This became a little strange, as I ended up pretending to check out some kind of weird fruit that I had never seen before. I reached out and felt one of them, acting as though I were an expert at picking out this particular type of fruit, but the truth of the matter was, I couldn't even pronounce the name that was written on the bright sign above it. Now, though, I was just three feet away from David's face, and I held my breath, wondering if he would recognize me.

"Hi, Grace," he said enthusiastically. "How are you?"

I glanced up, pretending that I hadn't noticed him until now and that I hadn't just completely orchestrated our running into each other, and arranged my facial expression into one of pleasant surprise. "I'm great; how are you?"

"I'm well," he replied, setting his produce in his cart. "So what are you up to this weekend?"

"Well, I was going to hang out with friends tonight, but no one was available, so I decided I would go grocery shopping instead," I answered, abandoning my perusal of the mysterious fruit. "I need to clean my house tomorrow and catch up on stuff for work, and then Sunday I'll be at church again." I cast my brightest smile at him.

"Your job makes you work at home on Saturdays? That's not very fair," he said, grinning in a potentially flirtatious manner. I wasn't sure. He was kind of difficult to interpret; he seemed like such a nice person that I couldn't tell if he was flirting or just being kind.

"Yeah, well…" I said, trailing off. I didn't have a good

comeback. I didn't want to be in a position in which I had to tell him what I did for a job. "What are you up to?"

"I always run all of my errands on Friday nights," he said. "It gives me a break from working on my sermon. Tomorrow I'll be putting finishing touches on it all day long. So I have to work on Saturday, too."

Hmmm, maybe I'll start running more of my errands on Friday nights in the hopes of bumping into him around town. I cringed. Had I seriously just considered planning my life around David's errands so that I might get to talk to him for two minutes every Friday? It was weird—half the time I thought I wanted to start dating Jake again, but ever since I had met David last Sunday I felt inexplicably drawn to spend time with him: it was like it was already more than a crush, even though I really didn't know him at all.

"Wow, well, I'll leave you to get on with all of that, then," I said. I didn't particularly want to leave, but I didn't want to overstay my welcome, either. It sounded as though he had a lot to do. I could talk to him again on Sunday. He was out of my league, anyway. How could something ever work out between a pastor and a woman who broke the law for her job? I mean, I personally didn't see anything wrong with my job—I was improving people's lives—but in all of my previous church experience, churchgoers were hardcore rule-followers who judged others when they didn't fit into their nice little pristine packages.

"Have a good night, Grace. I'll see you on Sunday," he said.

"Yeah, see you on Sunday." I left the produce section to grab other essentials, like toilet paper and rice milk. I wished that I had been able to come up with something to say that could have prolonged mine and David's conversation, but five minutes later, I still hadn't thought of anything. This was the problem: typical questions, like about careers and what one likes to do for fun, always ended up being turned back around to oneself, and I didn't like sharing with people that I was a bioenergetic practitioner and that for fun I spent a lot of time reading about alternative treatments for diabetes and MS and why it was a bad idea to get vaccines. That was probably why when I had tried to think of friends who I could hang out with this evening, the only people I could come up with were Jake, Candace, and Keisha. They were the only friends I had left who knew about my career and accepted me in spite of it. I supposed I hadn't really given my other friends a chance to get used to the idea that I broke the law in a large way on a regular basis; I had simply been too afraid to tell them, and so I just avoided the problem altogether. Most of the time I didn't think about it, but now I suddenly realized that my career, should I choose to continue in it, was going to play a large part in any future romantic relationships and friendships. Although this was something I should have picked up on sooner, I just now felt the loss of a thousand friendships, past, present, and future. There were going to be many who wouldn't accept me because of what I felt called to do. Maybe I really should try to get something started with Jake again—get off the fence on the issue and go for it. He accepted me for who I was, and I didn't have to explain anything. I was comfortable around him.

# # #

While I was at a stoplight a few miles from my house, my mom called. I answered cheerfully—after my reflection on the matter of acceptance, I was glad to hear from her and grateful that even though my parents did not wholly support my life-style, they still loved me and rarely tried to argue me out of it.

"Hon, I have some bad news," she said.

The light changed to green, and I lingered too long. Adults impatient to drive to broken families and second-mortgaged houses honked rudely. The person in the van directly behind me even tried to crawl his vehicle around my car, getting stuck halfway when he realized there wasn't enough space between the curb and my car for him to get all the way through without taking out both his side mirror and mine. This was completely out of character for me, but I raised my hand and flipped him off. And then I stayed right where I was. "What, Mom?"

"Dad, your aunts, and your uncle all decided to get tested for pancreatic cancer, since the doctor thought Grandpa's cancer could be hereditary. Dad's and Aunt Toni's tests both came back negative, but Aunt Kate and Uncle Mark tested positive. Aunt Kate's is nearly as far along as Grandpa's. There's probably not much they're going to be able to do."

The van driver had backed up and unbuckled his seatbelt and was now getting out of his vehicle with an extremely angry expression on his face. I jerked to attention and zipped around the corner recklessly, not responding to my mother. After I'd driven a mile or so and did not see the van following me, I relaxed slightly and managed to say calmly, "So that's pretty high odds that the rest of the family could develop pancreatic cancer at some point then, huh?"

I could tell my mom was crying but she controlled herself enough to answer, "Yes. Oh, Grace, it's bad enough that Grandpa has it, but now your aunt and uncle too?! Your dad was the first to get tested after Grandpa's diagnosis, and when Dad's returned negative, it gave the rest of the family some hope that maybe it wasn't genetic after all. But now it seems like it would be a good idea for your cousins to get tested." She paused. "Grace, you really should get tested, too."

I thought back to a distant mention of my great-grandfather, who had died after a short illness when he was in his forties. They had not performed an autopsy, but now it was apparent that he had probably died of pancreatic cancer.

I avoided her last statement. "Well, you already know this, but if any of them would like some help, I'll do whatever I can to help them. Free tests, the best products I can get my hands on…"

"That's kind of you, Grace, but I don't know if any of them would be open to it."

Sadly, if my own dad had tested positive, I didn't think even he would come to me for help. I was so grateful that his test had turned out negative.

"How's Dad doing?"

"He's been spending a lot of time with Grandpa; that's where he is right now. He doesn't say much about it, just does whatever he can to help Grandma and Grandpa. Yesterday he took Grandpa to a lawyer to work on his will. That was pretty hard for all of us." She sniffed.

I pulled into my garage and turned the car off, pulling my house key from my purse and unlocking the door connecting the house to the garage, plastic bags of groceries weighing my arms down. I stepped inside and kicked off my shoes, then headed to the kitchen to put the food away.

"Listen, Grace, if you can get here to visit everybody sometime soon, that would be really great. We have no idea how much time Grandpa and Kate have left."

"Mom, I have to go. I'll call you back later." I clicked my phone shut out of habit, staring at the mess that was my kitchen. Cupboard doors were thrust open, canned food rolling around on the countertop and floor, dishes strewn haphazardly across the place—some broken, some still whole. My living room was untouched. I ran around the house to check big-ticket items, like my TV, jewelry, and the desktop computer in my bedroom. All present. It occurred to me that I should check my special cabinet, and I flew down the stairs to my office.

CHAPTER FIFTEEN

Panicky, I ran downstairs and found the cabinet's heavy oak doors flung wide open, shelves bare. An open bottle of Eskaloft rolled around on the floor, its sand-colored capsules spilling out onto the carpet. I tried to calculate the cost of what had been in the cabinet, but when I reached three thousand dollars, I stopped adding. I couldn't bear to think of everything I had lost. It suddenly clicked as to why the thief had gone through my kitchen cupboards—I knew that if I checked, my personal supply of remedies would be missing as well. I couldn't report the break-in because obviously the police would ask what was stolen.

What if the thief was still in the house? The left-behind bottle suggested that the person had been interrupted. I jumped to attention, spinning around and studying the room immediately behind me. Jake's office door was closed, and I couldn't remember if he had shut it before he left for the day or not. I studied Keisha's tidy desk warily, nearly convincing myself that I could hear someone moving around under there. I would never feel comfortable staying here tonight unless I could know for sure that there wasn't someone watching. Likewise, I did not feel comfortable with the idea of going through my house by myself, checking for any sign that someone was still there. But who should I call? Probably the best option would be my parents, and it would probably even be a good idea for me to stay overnight with them (since fear would most likely keep me awake in my own house), but I didn't want to give them one more thing to worry about. They already had so many things to be anxious about with my family's health issues right now that I thought it best not to involve them in this situation. Plus, it would give them another reason to tell me to switch jobs, and that was not a conversation I was looking forward to right now.

I momentarily thought about my other options. I wanted to call Jake. I could have picked Candace, but she would not have made me feel any safer. She would have freaked out even more than I already was. I remembered that Jake had said that he had plans tonight, but this truly was an emergency and affected his business as well.

There was a lot of background noise when Jake picked up his phone—voices and loud thuds. "Where are you?"

"I'm at the bowling alley," he answered. "What's up?"

Good. If he was at the bowling alley closest to my house, he could be here in ten minutes. "I've got a problem. Someone broke into my house and stole all of our supplements."

I had his attention now. "What?! Grace, are you all right?"

"Yeah, I was at the grocery store when it happened. Whoever it was didn't take anything else, or so it seems."

"What can I do?" he asked.

Someone yelled "Strike!" and I waited for the manly cheering to calm down before I answered. "I was wondering if you could walk through my house with me and make sure there's not anyone here," I said timidly. Now that I was essentially asking Jake to be my protector, I felt stupid, like I was a little girl asking her daddy to check the closet for monsters.

There was a long pause, and I wondered why. I knew I shouldn't have asked him. "Never mind, Jake, I— "

"I'll be there in a few minutes."

"Thanks." I decided to wait outside and ended up taking out my frustration on yard work.

"Grace, what kind of an operation are you running in there, anyway?" My neighbor, Kurt, usually kept his distance, but apparently he was thinking a little too much today. He had wandered into my driveway and was watching me pull quack grass and two-inch-tall trees from my flowerbed.

I jumped at the sound of his voice. Who knew how long he had been standing there, eyeing me like a creeper. I self-consciously reached behind me, pulling my shirt down further over the back of my jeans, and squinted up at him. He was dressed in khaki shorts and a bright pink polo shirt, graying hair perfectly gelled and expensive sunglasses hiding the crow's feet in the corners of his eyes.

"Hi, Kurt." I threw a dandelion into the small pile of uprooted flowerbed fakers and swiped a hand across the sweat beading on my upper lip. "What, exactly, are you referring to?"

He scratched nervously behind his ear. Kurt never showed anxiety; strangely enough, the fact that he looked so uncomfortable made me calm down.

"Well, I just wondered…are you growing marijuana or cooking meth or something? You sure have a lot of people coming and going from your house all the time."

I laughed. "No, Kurt, I'm not selling drugs." *Not the kind you're thinking of.*

He looked disappointed. "Oh, okay, well, I just thought I'd ask. Never mind."

A familiar Jeep pulled into my driveway, and I quickly excused myself. Kurt walked back across the street to his house, glancing over his shoulder a couple of times as if to make sure that Jake wasn't there to pick up some weed.

I was startled to see that someone was with Jake—a woman—and she looked like…Chrystina. It suddenly dawned on me that the reason he had been so vague about his plans for the evening was because it was a date. A date with the cop I had laughed at for slipping him her phone number. A cop who could easily collapse the wobbling security of our lives in an instant and who I was especially suspicious of for showing up so many times supposedly by coincidence.

My eyes narrowed, and I hesitated in the grass, no longer quite so eager to see my hero. It didn't bother me exactly that he was on a date with someone—it was more like I was concerned as to what Chrystina was up to. At least I didn't think it bothered me that he was on a date. I didn't *want* it to bother me.

Jake and Chrystina both climbed out, and Jake rushed over to me but didn't provide the reassuring hug I was hoping for. "Grace, are you okay? Do you really think someone's still in there?"

Chrystina had pulled out her gun and was heading toward my front door. I wasn't sure where she kept the thing—she wouldn't have been able to fit it inside the skin-tight, low-cut black Henley, and her denim mini-skirt didn't appear to have extra room. Maybe she strapped the gun to her thigh. How sexy of her. How did she bowl in that outfit? I rolled my eyes.

"I don't think there's anyone in there, but I was too scared to stay inside and check for myself," I said. Chrystina seemed to be enough out of earshot that I felt it safe to ask Jake, "What are you doing with *her*? I really don't think it's a good idea for her to be involved in this situation." I wanted to add, *Or in your life at all*, but kept that comment to myself since he had dropped everything to help me out.

Jake didn't provide me with an answer to the question, instead responding curtly, "Don't worry, I didn't tell her what was taken; I just said that your house had been broken into." Then he walked inside.

I scurried after them, realizing that I needed to clean up the Eskaloft before Chrystina saw it. After I had run downstairs and kicked the bottle and its spilled pills into the dark, dusty cave underneath the armoire, I joined the unlikely couple in my kitchen. The house was darkening now, and through the window over my sink I could see the moon beginning to shine brightly. Everything in the house was cast in shadow, and I was suddenly aware of the smell of burnt macaroni from my lunch. A moonbeam glinted off the silvery-white buttons on Chrystina's shirt, and I also glimpsed a coat of dust on one of the paintings on my wall. The cop and her devoted fan were looking at the sliding glass door that led out onto my deck. "Grace, I think this is how the person came in," Chrystina said. "This door isn't locked."

She was probably right. I did my best to keep my house secured but frequently forgot to lock this door.

"Is there anything missing?" she pressed.

I glanced over at Jake and lied. "Doesn't seem to be. My house is just trashed."

"Strange," Chrystina commented. "Do you have any enemies who would want to hurt you by damaging your belongings? First your car, now your house."

Enemies? Ha. I'd say she was my worst one right now. Other than Chrystina, though, I couldn't think of anybody who posed a threat, let alone someone who knew about my secret stash and would feel the need to steal it from me.

"I can get some people over here to dust for prints and stuff," Chrystina said, whipping out her cell phone.

"No, no, that's all right," I quickly reassured her. I didn't want more police snooping around my house. "I don't think whoever it was took anything, so let's let it go for now."

Chrystina tilted her head and raised her eyebrows at me. "Are you sure? That's not the typical response."

"I know, I just…" I assembled an excuse out of the mush in my brain. "I have a lot going on right now, and I feel like it would be more stressful having cops over to check the place out than it would be just to let it go, especially since nothing's missing." *Except for thousands of dollars of illegal supplements.*

"I have to let the station know." Chrystina slowly folded her phone back up and tucked her gun into the waistband of her skirt. "We've been keeping an eye on this neighborhood for several days now. We suspected that something weird was going on."

I thought back to when she had shown up at my house and questioned me about Suzanne. But Suzanne would have had absolutely nothing to do with this. Suzanne was one of my nicest, most loyal clients.

"I can file a report later, I guess," Chrystina said reluctantly. "I'll just tell them you don't want to press charges. I'll go make sure no one is in your basement."

Jake followed her downstairs while I sank onto a bar stool, uncertain how to cope with everything that was going on. I could hear them moving around in the basement, and I wondered exactly what Jake was telling Chrystina about the offices that were clearly set up in the various rooms.

Eventually the two left, and I was alone in my house. It was completely dark by now, and I continued to sit in the kitchen. Every sound made my heart buck wildly—the hum of the refrigerator, the chirp of the crickets outside, Kurt's German Shepherd whining—and I turned around to study the living room behind me every two or three minutes, certain that I felt eyes focused on my back. I reached the point that I was so on edge from the grip of fear that I began to pack a bag to take to my parents' home. Much as I didn't want to worry them, there was no way I could stay in the house by myself all night.

I was cramming cosmetics into a plastic bag when my cell rang, my tightly-wound nerves coiling even tighter from the unexpected noise, causing pain in my neck and shoulders. Jake.

"Grace, are you doing okay?" he asked quietly.

"No," I said, crying softly with the relief that it was just my cell and it was just Jake.

"Would you like me to come sleep on your couch tonight? Would that make you feel better to know that someone else is in the house?"

"Yes. Jake, you're amazing." I slid my bag to the floor and stretched out across my bed, already beginning to feel the tension dissipate. "Thank you."

CHAPTER SIXTEEN

Jake's promise to come over greatly aided my mental health. I fearlessly conquered the mess the vandal had left in my kitchen, throwing broken dishes away and trying to look at the task as an opportunity to clean out and organize my cupboards, which truthfully had been getting rather cluttered. When Jake arrived, he assisted by vacuuming up minuscule shards of glass and wiping down my countertops.

"I think that's all." He moved so that I could shut the last cupboard doors, but I tripped over his foot, and suddenly we were standing incredibly close to each other. He grasped my upper arms to steady me and then reached up further and rubbed my neck and shoulders. "How's your back? I haven't worked on you in a while. Do you need an adjustment? You feel really tense."

Warm memories from our past relationship flooded into my mind and body, and I briefly relaxed into his touch. It had been a really bad night, and what could it hurt to let him adjust my back and maybe give me a quick massage? It wasn't going to lead to anything…maybe it would if I wanted it to…but no, he was just here to keep me safe or at least create the illusion of safety so that I could get some sleep…"I…um…maybe just a quick adjustment."

The basement was slightly cold as we walked down to his office. It was like a slap in the face as I suddenly remembered his date with Chrystina. He hadn't mentioned it again at all. Was Jake really as much of a womanizer as he seemed to be? He could be so nice, and yet sometimes, like right now, I just had to wonder if everything was about sex for him. Yeah, I know he's a guy and that's supposedly all they think about, but there had to be someone out there who wasn't so manipulative. Or maybe Jake wasn't manipulative and I was judging him unfairly. I couldn't decide. I had ruined his night with Chrystina, but one woman could easily substitute for another, right? He was working on wearing me down. And I somehow still wanted to believe that things would work out between us.

I lay on my stomach on the padded chiropractic table, face down in between white tissue covering leather. Jake carefully, expertly, felt my spine with both hands. "Relax, Grace," he whispered when he pushed down hard on a spot on my back and it refused to be coaxed into place.

I shivered.

His warm palms spread out over my back, rubbing gently across my shoulders and working down, down, nearly to my hips. My body felt as though it were meshed with the table, and this time Jake was able to move my back with me barely even aware that he was doing so.

It was so clinical, and yet at the same time I don't think either of us was exactly sure what we wanted to get out of it. Chrystina popped into my thoughts, and I pushed her away again. Finally, though, I felt that I had to say something. "Jake, what's up with you and that cop?"

His fingers paused, and I could sense the thoughts tracking through his brain, could tell that he was trying to decide whether to lie or not. For whatever reason, I wasn't even angry that there was a strong possibility that he was going to lie to me. I was so exhausted from everything that had been going on lately, and there was a large part of me that didn't want to know if he and Chrystina were getting along well, if they were planning to hang out again, if maybe they had even been in contact with each other frequently ever since the day my car exploded.

Jake cleared his throat. "I gave her a call a while ago."

Made sense that I wouldn't know about it. My illness had taken up much of my time lately. Until recently, I hadn't been aware of much that was going on, other than that I could hardly swallow. I thought of the phone call Jake had taken when he ate lunch with Keisha and me and wondered if he had been talking to Chrystina then.

"Chrystina seemed excited to talk to me and mentioned that she was in town—she remembered where I lived from when she pulled us over and had to look at my license. We talked for a while, and I asked if she wanted to get together. Tonight was the first night that both of us have had free to hang out."

The question that had been rolling around in my brain ever since Chrystina and her partner appeared at my door to interrogate me about Suzanne popped out of my mouth. "But,

Jake, don't you think it's weird that she was in North Carolina and that she's in our town all of a sudden?" I had turned over onto my back and stared up at him.

"I don't know, I just assumed she's on vacation here or something," Jake replied, shrugging his shoulders.

Had I really not mentioned to him that she had come by my house? I had no idea how I had forgotten to tell him that important piece of information. "She definitely appeared in uniform at my front door a while ago, asking about one of my clients."

Jake didn't seem nearly as startled or worried as I thought he should be. "Well, I don't know. Maybe she moved here."

"It's weird, Jake. I don't like the situation." I sat up. Our close moment was over, and I knew that was for the best. "What did you talk about all night, anyway? It's not like you can tell her about your job, and apparently she didn't talk about whether she's working in North Carolina or here right now."

"I had just picked her up like half an hour before you called," Jake said. "We had just started bowling; we were on the third frame when you called about the break-in."

I wanted to smile so badly when he confirmed my suspicion that I had disturbed their time together, but I held it back.

He sat down in a chair across the room, rubbing his forehead. "So what should we do about the stolen products?"

"I guess I'm going to have to smuggle it all in again sooner than I'd planned." The very thought made my heart race. Even though last time had gone well (minus the car explosion and tension with Jake), this time would be trickier, as I would probably have to go out of the country. I did have my passport now, so I was grateful for that at least. "You up for another trip?"

"Of course," he said. "It *has* to go better than last time."

I nodded.

After an awkward minute of silence, we agreed that it had been a long day and it was probably best for both of us to go to sleep, even though it was still only 9 p.m. I was lying awake in my bed by 9:15, Jake on the couch in my living room, and all I felt was confusion.

# # #

I'd decided to go a bit more casual this Sunday and dressed in my newest pair of jeans with a sleeveless, glittery, flowy top and a black, cap-sleeved blazer. I also decided to be a bit more daring and sat a few rows closer to David than I had the previous week. His back was to me, and I kept watching him, waiting for the moment he would turn around and I could wave.

Until Valerie approached me again, that is.

"Grace! I'm glad you came back! Do you want to sit with me and a couple of my friends?"

Are you sitting closer to David or farther away? was what I wanted to ask. "Sure."

Valerie led me to the opposite side of the church and several rows back, where "a couple" of her friends translated into six people, not including Valerie or me. "Hey, guys, this is Grace. She's new. Grace, this is Amy, Sherri, Sherri's boyfriend Scott, Lauryn, Michelle, and Michelle's boyfriend Derek."

Five of the six faces smiled back at me—Lauryn looked dangerously close to asking me to step into the corner and die. At least she was in the middle and I wouldn't have to sit next to her.

Once again, there was a large variety of people present for the service. I decided to try to be outgoing and introduced myself to the homeless-looking couple, Jim and Joan Alfieri, after church. We were in the midst of a discussion about how much they liked Charleston Community when Pastor David approached our tiny group.

He stuck out his hand for me. "Grace, I'm glad to see you came back. Jim, Joan, always great to see you two as well. How's everything going?"

Jim and Joan talked for a couple of minutes while I stood by silently, trying hard to listen but getting distracted by David's close proximity to my elbow. David's nearness coupled with Jim's lisp left me unable to pay attention to much more than Jim's every third sentence or so. I jumped when someone gently tapped my shoulder.

"Grace, would you like to join us at Panera for lunch?" Valerie asked quietly when I turned. Her friends were clustered behind her.

"I, uh…" Oh, who was I kidding? Nothing was ever going to become of me and David, anyway. I may as well get better acquainted with other people in the church. "Sounds great."

I silently waved good-bye with a smile to all of the participants in the previous conversation and made my way to the parking lot.

Panera Bread was bustling with activity and delicious smells when I opened the door and peered in for a familiar face. Valerie and the others were already in line and motioned for me to join them. I looked at the several people lined up behind my new-found church buddies and felt bad cutting, so I opted to tag on to the end of the line. I was peering at the menu, trying to figure out my healthiest option, when a male voice whispered, "If you're having a hard time deciding, their broccoli cheese soup is always a safe bet."

I smiled, recognizing the voice, and turned around. "Thanks for the advice. How's their chicken noodle?"

"Also a good choice." David nodded enthusiastically. "Honestly, I've tried about two-thirds of the menu, and it's all good. Haven't you ever eaten here before?"

"I don't eat out much. Restaurants add a lot of extra chemicals to their food."

"Health nut, huh?" To my surprise, he said this admiringly.

"Yeah."

"More power to you. I go in healthy streaks, but for the most part I end up eating whatever I want. My self-discipline in that area is next to nothing." He grinned. "I'm a sucker for a chocolate chip cookie or just about anything homemade, really."

I mentally filed this information away, thinking that maybe I could make him my grandma's amazing chocolate chunk cookie recipe, which was a total joke because I bake about once every two years. *But I would bake for David.* I was falling too hard, too fast. *Regroup, Grace, get yourself together.* "So who are you eating with here?"

"My sister, actually. She's driven down from Grand Rapids to hang out for the afternoon."

"That's cool." *Good sign. Gets along well with his family and is not here on a date.*

"Hey, are you busy this coming Saturday? I have this mission project thing going on and I'm trying to recruit people to help. We could catch some dinner beforehand, if you want." He looked a little nervous, like he was asking me on a date. But if it was a group of people, it totally wasn't a date, right?

"That sounds great." I noticed that, sadly, the line had moved up and I was going to have to make a decision about my food quickly. I pulled paper out of my purse and wrote out my phone number. "Here's my number, if you want to give me a call with details later in the week."

"Fantastic! Thanks, Grace." He looked overjoyed. It had been a long time since I'd seen any guy that excited over something I'd said or done, and I silently reminded myself once again that it was not going to be a date.

CHAPTER SEVENTEEN

Over the next few days, I was able to connect with Candace and a few other bioenergetic practitioner friends of ours to warn them about the break-in. Candace decided that she was going to transfer her remedies into a fire-proof safe. All of the people that I contacted were quite generous and offered to sell me some of their products to get my business through until I would be able to go on a road trip again. I dug into my savings account and visited each of these friends at their houses, picking up approximately $300 worth of supplements from each. It wasn't much altogether, but it was far better than the nothing the vandal had left me with, and I was grateful.

Saturday afternoon I panicked. I had an angry client call *and* I had to get ready for my half-date.

"Kim, it's a Herxheimer reaction. Remember? I told you this would probably happen. You're just cleansing too fast. Drink lots of water, rest up for a couple of days, and you'll be fine. Your body is just overloaded with toxins right now, and that's what's causing all of your problems. I promise, you're not dying, but you need to drink as much water as possible so that the toxins don't re-settle somewhere else in your body. Back off on all of your homeopathics and pills and everything, just until you're feeling better."

"I don't know, maybe I should go to the ER," Kim Christopherson hedged. "My brother is a doctor, and he thinks my symptoms could indicate that I need some new medications and that I might even be in bad enough shape to be hospitalized for a while."

"Kim, I know, and I can't make your decisions for you, of course, but if you just stick this out, I think you'll be able to get off your prescription meds completely. Look at how far you've come in the past few months!"

She interrupted me. "Grace, I appreciate your help, but my brother doesn't think it's done me much good. I wasn't really calling to ask for your advice; it's more like I'm calling to tell you that I'm going to be finished with your program. Goodbye."

She hung up on me.

Not only was I offended by the hang-up and the lack of trust in my medical abilities, but now I had a pressing concern that Kim might slip up and unknowingly turn me in to the authorities via her brother. I trusted her enough to know that she probably wouldn't do it on purpose, of course, but words could slip out and have nasty consequences.

Now I had something to mull over while preparing for my date. Keisha had to know all the details, of course, and gave me her advice as to what jewelry I should wear with my new outfit. I had ended up selecting new khakis and a slightly dressy top while shopping with Candace—I wanted to look nice yet was unsure as to what type of work the mission project was going to entail. David had told me where we would be going to dinner but had received an urgent phone call while on the phone with me and had neglected to tell me any details about the mission project.

"Stop worrying," Jake told me. He had grown far more relaxed toward the dangers of his job, almost too much so, since beginning to date the policewoman. "Kim's not going to turn you in. She's smarter than that. And nicer than that."

I didn't say anything to that comment. As far as I knew, he still hadn't told Chrystina about his career yet, and if I opened my mouth at all, I knew I would confront him about that aspect of his relationship. Not a good time.

I curled my hair but pulled it back in a low ponytail so as not to over-do it.

Dinner was uneventful. David decided, though, that he would keep the mission project a secret.

I only pestered him with a few questions about the project but felt my heart sink when I saw that we were pulling into the hospital parking lot. What was going on?

The oldies station playing quietly on the radio morphed into the news as we slid into a new half-hour. David reached over and turned the volume up. "I want to hear the weather report before we go in. I'm supposed to go golfing on Monday," he explained.

"A crowd gathered outside the Simmons County Jail today to protest the detaining of Dr. Carl Bateman, an acupuncturist in Portland. There was no violence, but the crowd was quite vocal about their testimonies in support of alternative health treatments. Many claim to be former patients of Dr. Bateman, while other protesters refuse to identify exactly how they are connected to the acupuncturist."

I was impressed that people would openly admit that they participated in alternative healing. There were punishments not only for alternative practitioners but also fines and even the possibility of jail time for their patients, depending on their level of involvement.

David and I listened to the rest of the news and the weather. "So what do you think about that mess going on with Dr. Bateman? Do you think he should be put in jail because of his occupation?" he inquired.

Here we go. "Well…I believe that people should be able to choose their own health treatments. I personally wish that the alternative medical community and the traditional medical community could just combine and work together for the good of sick people everywhere, you know? So, no, I don't think the acupuncturist should be punished at all for helping people feel better. It's not like he's Kevorkian, killing people off. He's dedicated his life to relieving pain for people without medications that are loaded with side effects, and he deserves to be allowed to continue his practice." *And I'm about to lose a new friend and have my opinion completely shot down in three…two…one…*

"Interesting perspective."

I waited for the argument that was sure to follow, but it never came.

"So, it's actually just going to be us," David said nervously as he parked his car. He must have realized that the previous conversation was not a good direction in which to head. "The other two people who were going to come backed out on me this afternoon. I, along with a couple of other members from Charleston Community, try to visit the sick people from church here every other week or so. I didn't want to give you any specific details too soon so that you could back out on me, but typically what we do to cheer them up is sing, sometimes hymns for the older people, but also really stupid songs sometimes, too, like from Backstreet Boys or even Britney Spears. Here, I'll show you."

He hopped out of the car and opened the trunk, pulling out a large cardboard box. The situation almost reminded me of mine and Jake's smuggling trip. I stepped out of the car as well, curious as to what he was lugging around in that box.

David grinned sheepishly, lifting wigs and glittery pieces of fabric from the depths of the mottled cardboard, "Walker Farms" printed diagonally across the side. "We usually, uh, dress up a little, too."

I smiled a little and raised my eyebrows, trying desperately to think of whether I should agree with him and go along with his crazy plan or back out to spare myself the embarrassment. He really should have warned me about this sooner. This was kind of an awkward thing to participate in on a half-date with someone you'd only known for two weeks.

I watched as the enthusiasm drained from his face bit by bit while I continued to remain silent. "I'm sorry, Grace, I never should have kept this a secret from you. You don't have to participate. In fact, I can take you home right now if you want, or I'm sure the hospital has some other area you could volunteer in—"

"Are you kidding me? Of course I'll do it! This sounds

really fun!" That came out of my mouth before I could stop it. He just looked so disappointed. I figured I would regret this decision and look back on this day as one full of awkwardness and shame, but it was too late now.

# # #

David's excitement over this strange mission project grew as we traversed elevators and squeaky-clean hallways to get to the first patient. "Now the first person we're visiting is Ron Ripley. He's in his early sixties, has been in and out of the hospital for the last few months for chemotherapy and surgeries, and I get the most laughs out of him when I sing Michael Jackson songs."

As a closet Michael Jackson fan, I considered pretending that I didn't know all of the lyrics to his top twenty hits, along with the majority of the lyrics to many of his other songs; but if I was already stooping to this level of embarrassment, why not belt out the songs with confidence?

We stopped outside Ron's room, and David set the box of accessories on the linoleum. "You can wear whatever you want," he whispered. "It doesn't necessarily have to be something that Michael Jackson would wear."

"You are too generous, sir," I quipped quietly. "How can I possibly select something to wear out of all of these fabulous choices?"

"Might I make a suggestion?" David returned. "How about this and this?" He held up a long, Cher-esque wig and the most hideous sequined jacket I had ever seen, complete with large, gaudy stars in all the colors of the rainbow.

"You have a tremendous sense of fashion," I teased, slipping into the jacket, which was stiff as a coat of armor from all the sequins. I took the wig and tried to put it on, but my real hair interfered and I ended up putting the wig on with the front off-kilter, sloping dramatically to the right side of my head.

David stopped me from fixing it. "It's way better this way."

I blew disgusting synthetic hair out of my mouth. "Yeah?"

"Definitely."

"What are you going to wear?"

"This special piece of work." David pulled out a Mohawk wig in a coppery red. Apparently it had been floating around in the box a little too long because a good three-inch section of the Mohawk was matted down and sticking out to the front instead of straight up. He put it on his head anyway before pulling on an orange bathrobe and an enormous leather vest over the top of that. Once he was wearing the wig, I could see that not only was it a Mohawk, but it also had a mullet in the back. Wow.

"They let you keep being the pastor despite all of this?" I asked in a playful way, although I was secretly thinking of how much this behavior would not have been acceptable at my old church. And how much fun the congregation missed out on because of all that legalism.

"I know, I can't really believe it, either," he said, pushing the box closer to the wall with his foot. "Now, I'm going to see if Ron is ready for us, and then we'll start the show."

"Wait, what are we singing?"

"What Michael Jackson songs do you at least know the chorus to?"

Too many. "Um, what ones do *you* know?" I dodged his

question with a question.

"You wanna do 'Beat It'? Or how about 'Bad'?"

"'Bad' has a really sweet music video," I answered. "I feel as though I would love to try out some of those moves right now."

"'Bad' it is, then."

And so began the absolute worst performance of my entire life. I actually had had some dance lessons as a child and teen, but this…this was bad. Ron thoroughly enjoyed it, though. I had thought that we were going to have to perform a capella, but after a couple of false starts, Ron whipped out a Michael Jackson CD from the drawer of his bedside table. Come to find out after we performed both "Bad" and "Thriller," Ron didn't like Michael Jackson's music all that much. He just liked to see David perform it and had asked his wife to buy the CD specifically for that purpose. We visited with Ron for a few minutes after our little karaoke session before moving on to the next patient. This time was easier; a woman in her nineties wanted us to sing some hymns with her. She must have asked my name six different times, but she had the words to "I'll Fly Away" and "It Is Well with My Soul" completely memorized.

As we walked to the third room, David briefed me quietly. "This next one's going to be quite a bit harder. This woman is in her twenties and has been in and out of the hospital fighting leukemia. The doctors have pretty much told her she's going to die within the next few months, and so she's been trying to live it up, staying out of the hospital as much as possible. Her attitude has really gone downhill lately, though, and I don't even know if she'll let us see her today."

So this time, instead of discussing beforehand what we would be doing for entertainment, we walked casually into the room and sat next to the bed of a person I was very surprised to see—bitter Lauryn from church.

She was hooked up to an IV and somewhat groggy, but Lauryn's scowl was firmly in place. She smiled a little at David, but I was definitely not welcome in her hospital room. I greeted her as though I didn't notice her unfriendliness, and David certainly didn't seem to pick up on the distinction between Lauryn's attitude toward me and her attitude toward him.

"Oh, have you two met before?" he inquired.

"We have," I answered quickly, before Lauryn could interject something negative. "At church last week. And then we both ate lunch at Panera with some other friends after church."

"Oh, okay," David replied. "Lauryn, how are you feeling today?"

Lauryn launched into a whiny monologue of her nausea, her pain, her blah, blah, blah. I tuned back in when she started talking about how unfair it was that God would do all of this to her. That God wouldn't just heal her. "After all," she argued, "I'm a good person. Really, why would He even bother letting people get sick at all?"

David took a deep breath, and I braced for a lengthy theological discussion. Instead, he said, "Lauryn, I don't really have any easy answers for you. But..."

"Sometimes I don't even think there's a God at all," she spat out.

Whoa. Whoa, whoa. Having seen her in church, I just assumed...well, one should never assume things without proof.

There is a way for you to get better, I wanted to say. *But I can't tell you because I'll get arrested. And I don't think you'd listen, anyway.*

As if she'd heard my thoughts, Lauryn continued, "My cousin tried to get me to try some alternative medicine crap, but no way was I going to try something illegal. My doctor said that stuff never works anyway. It's just a bunch of weirdos trying to get your money for cheap herbs."

I bit my tongue.

"Lauryn, is there anything we can do for you?" David asked gently. "Is it all right if we pray for you right now?"

"I can't really stand hearing prayers that I know aren't going to be answered," she replied. "I don't care if you pray on your own time, but I don't want to hear it. Sorry, Pastor."

Lauryn was making me so incredibly angry with her poorly-informed opinion of alternative treatments and her horrible attitude about life in general that I couldn't stand it any longer. I walked out of the room.

CHAPTER EIGHTEEN

I walked to the end of the hallway, realizing once I had left Lauryn's room that I couldn't actually go anywhere because I was depending on David for a ride. I paced in a small box for a short while, balling my hands into fists and running the ends of my pointer fingers across my sharp thumbnails, ragged from stress-picking, digging so hard that I nearly cut myself. *I want to get out of here.* Not only did I feel attacked by Lauryn but also overwhelmed by even being in a hospital. The hospital represented everything that hated me—not everything that I hated, but everything that hated *me.* Kim's decision earlier, Lauryn's anger…I even felt as though Jake hated me, not because he had said so, but because he would risk the success of our careers by starting a relationship with Chrystina.

I liked David, but maybe he was just too spiritual for me, and I didn't think I would ever be able to handle this hospital mission work with him again. Maybe my decision to start going back to church was wrong. Maybe I didn't need to re-connect with God. Maybe it was all a bunch of lies to get you to pay your money to the church. I didn't know, and I wasn't sure if I cared anymore.

I had just buttoned up my coat and was preparing to call someone to pick me up—I wasn't sure who, but I was thinking maybe Keisha because she lived the closest—when David walked out of the room. I blew past him. "I'm going to take off, David."

He caught my sleeve and I stopped only because I didn't want to tear this coat; it was my favorite. "Can I just talk to you for a minute, Grace?" He didn't sound the least bit irritated, only concerned. "I'm sorry if Lauryn upset you." I could tell he wanted to know why she had made me so angry, but he didn't ask, and I respected him for it.

"Thanks, I guess." I shrugged out of his grasp. "You really don't need to apologize for what comes out of someone else's mouth, though."

He didn't say anything. Just waited.

Was it safe to tell him about my secret life? I felt like I could trust him, but I didn't really know him well at all. As a pastor, he might feel that he needed to report me to the police in order to keep his own conscience clear. I was so tired of keeping everything a secret from everybody, though. "I can't talk about it here."

He nodded. "Fair enough. Where do you want to go?"

I thought for a minute. Nowhere was safe, so... "The park?"

"Okay."

He bought us hot chocolate, and we sat on a damp bench. The park was deserted at this time of day. The swings creaked in the wind, and occasionally a drop of water would fall onto my head from the maples above. I took a deep breath and spilled my guts. David was the perfect listener; he didn't even ask any questions for quite a while after I had finished.

"Wow. That takes a lot of courage, Grace," he eventually stated. "I don't think I could do it."

"Tell another person about it or do the job itself?"

"Sacrifice myself every day like that for the health of virtual strangers, knowing that at any point I could be discovered and spend time in jail for it. I'm pretty attached to my freedom." He smiled. "I definitely understand now why Lauryn made you so angry. Let me ask you something…what do you believe about God, Grace?"

I blushed. I was completely unprepared for a question like this. "I…well, I…I'm trying to get back into going to church regularly." I didn't tell him that I was now thinking about giving this up.

"That's great, but God is different than church…" he said carefully.

"Oh, of course. I know. When I was little, I attended church with my parents a lot, and we all believed the whole 'one way to heaven' thing. I haven't given it much thought in years. I mean, I don't know. I believe that Jesus came to earth, died for our sins, and rose again. What more is there?" I felt a little flippant with that last question but couldn't take it back now.

He studied a thunderhead rolling our way. "A lot more, actually. God wants us to spend time getting to know him. Life doesn't have to be about just getting by, occasionally thinking about how great heaven will be."

I was too embarrassed to admit it, but usually my thoughts about heaven were not good ones. I mean, I knew it was a much better option than hell, but I didn't dwell on heaven in the friendliest of terms. I always pictured sitting around on clouds, playing a harp. It sounded horrifically boring.

"You'd be surprised at how interesting life can be if you really commit to developing a relationship with God," David continued. "You know, reading the Bible and praying and stuff. He'll give you more of a desire for it the more time you spend doing it."

"Hmm," I replied intelligently.

And just like that, he dropped the subject. "So, Grace, will you test me?"

# # #

We drove back to my house. I was really going to do it. I was going to show this man who could easily turn me in exactly how my bioenergetic program worked and even show him where I kept my stash of supplements. The closer we got to my house, the more a look of uneasiness grew on his face. I was unaccustomed to this mood. Even through the thing with Lauryn and then my outburst, he had never looked so unhappy.

"Is something wrong?" I asked while starting up a new file for him on my laptop.

"Grace, there's something I should probably tell you before you get started with the test." His gaze focused on the bookshelf behind me, rather than on my face.

I tried to act nonchalant, like nothing he could possibly

say would upset me. "What's that?" Was he about to tell me he was secretly with the police or something?

"Well, I don't know how it's going to come up on the test, but there's the possibility that I might...have AIDS."

I didn't say anything—wasn't sure what to say to that at all. I had never had a person with AIDS come to me before for help, let alone someone that I cared about so much tell me that he might have it.

"I haven't been to the doctor in a good three or four years because I didn't want to know. They say the AIDS virus can lie dormant in your body for years, and I haven't been sick or anything. But a few years ago, I was driving on the expressway and a really bad accident happened right in front of me. I was a campus paramedic for two years in college, so since I was right there, I decided to stop and help in whatever way I could until an ambulance could get there. Both people in the car were bleeding a lot, and as I was trying to open up the car door to help them, some of the metal that had pulled away from the frame cut me. I didn't pay much attention to it—I was too focused on helping them, and even though I knew better than to get mixed up in all that blood, I just wanted to save their lives if I could. Anyway, when the paramedics showed up, I heard them asking the injured woman, who was slightly awake, some questions, and I heard her say that her husband had AIDS. I looked down at myself, covered in his blood, my own cut beginning to bleed pretty badly, and I freaked out. I walked away, drove away from the scene, and spent the next few weeks debating whether I should go to the doctor and get tested or not. I decided that I didn't want to know, and since I don't sleep around, I decided just to let things be. I probably should have gone in and been tested right away, but I was scared. As far as I know, I don't have any symptoms, but like I said earlier, the symptoms can lie dormant for a long time."

Suddenly I wasn't so eager to share my abilities with the pastor. Now that this was no longer a "normal" type of test but rather one that could drastically affect his life, I didn't have much desire to continue. *Wouldn't it be better for him not to know?* I wondered. *I mean, he's made it this far in life without getting tested. He's not sick or anything. Probably he doesn't have AIDS.* I knew, though, that the odds of him not having it were pretty slim after his exposure to the virus. And...I knew I shouldn't even be thinking this, considering that we weren't really dating at this point, but...what if we got into a really serious relationship? In that case, I would want to know if he had AIDS or not, because I definitely didn't want to contract it. And I owed it to whatever woman he married someday to help him face his fear of finding out if he had AIDS or not.

"Grace, I'm sorry. I shouldn't have unloaded all that baggage on you." David looked vastly uncomfortable with having spilled his deepest secret. I wondered if he had told anyone else all of this before and decided that might be the safest thing that I could say next.

"David, does anyone else know...?"

"My closest friend, a pastor that I attended college with, knows. He's the only other person I've ever told."

I nodded in acknowledgment. This was some heavy stuff. I suddenly wished that Jake was just next door in his office and that I could pull him in on this impromptu appointment. He usually knew what to say in situations like this. But, alas, Jake was spending time with his girlfriend.

"Are you sure you want to go through with the test?" my voice cracked out.

"It's time. I've got to, Grace. This has held such a huge grip over my life, and I need to find out the truth so that I can continue on, whatever the outcome is." He looked like he was about to cry.

"Okay." I positioned his hand on the cradle. "I do need to tell you up front that I'm not considered a medical doctor, so what I tell you is not an official diagnosis. What I tell you will be what my computer indicates you have."

"I understand that," he said.

The initial test took just a few minutes. I was devastated, but not exactly surprised, to discover the truth. It was the hardest thing I had ever had to tell any of my clients.

"David, I'm sorry. You do have AIDS."

CHAPTER NINETEEN

I was sick again that night after David left. A fear that had been hovering in the back of my mind rose to the surface and I was finally forced to consider the idea that since so many members of my family had been diagnosed with pancreatic cancer, there was a chance that I could have it, too. In the midst of all the busyness, it had been close to a year since I had tested myself or asked someone else to test me. I had assumed all along that my frequent illness was from stress (which was still a possibility), but what if something else was lurking in my body, growing and taking over? I had a tremendous amount of faith in the ability of supplements and good nutrition to eradicate cancer, but for some reason I was still scared and created all kinds of reasons why I should wait to get tested.

Four long days passed. I found David's email address printed in a church bulletin and sent him some links to several websites about alternative health options—some were about AIDS specifically, while others were just about holistic health in general—my efforts to get him to try my side of things.

David and I had talked on the phone only occasionally since the discovery of his disease. He still was not experiencing any symptoms, so he had some doubts (understandably) about the test results. I figured he was trying to keep his fears at bay—it only made sense. It was the same thing I was doing. In my spare time, I read up on various ways to fight AIDS but kept returning to the one that I had found the previous month. Hulda Clark, a well-known doctor in the field of alternative health practices, had written a book in the mid-nineties called *The Cure for HIV and AIDS*, proposing that parasites and the solvent benzene were at the root of the HIV virus and the AIDS condition. If one followed her procedures to rid these contaminants from the body, then that person could become free of HIV/AIDS. It was quite encouraging, especially since I was planning another smuggling trip soon and knew that I would probably be able to obtain the herbs that would help to kill the parasites. If everything went according to plan, and if David was open to trying these remedies, he could easily be AIDS-free within a couple of months.

I didn't want to nag him about the situation, but the topic kept coming up when we actually did talk, and I could tell he was really confused and uncertain about what to do. What I had originally feared seemed to have happened—my career and weird beliefs had pushed him away. At any rate, I wasn't sure what direction I wanted the relationship to go after I found out that he had AIDS. I didn't want to be discriminatory or anything, but I certainly didn't want AIDS, and if he wasn't willing to do something to get rid of it—well, then, as long as he promised to keep his mouth shut to the authorities about my business, then maybe it was best that we cut off any relationship we had—even friendship—now. I could find someone else, I consoled myself. It wasn't the end of the world. I was only twenty-six; I had plenty of time to find someone. And then he called me.

It had been six days since I'd heard from him at all. I'd skipped church last week on account of being sick again.

"Grace?"

"Hey."

"I think I want to try it—that AIDS cure you told me about. I'm going to need a lot of help, though. I don't understand much of any of this healthy stuff. But I want this to stop hanging over my head. I want to try my best to get rid of it."

I smiled. I couldn't even begin to imagine how hard this could be for him. But it gave him a lot more hope than he could possibly have if he didn't do anything about his situation.

# # #

To celebrate their three-month anniversary, Jake took Chrystina on a week-long trip to Vegas. During their absence, I decided that I had to confront Jake as soon as the opportunity presented itself. To the best of my knowledge, he had continued to keep his job a secret from his girlfriend, and they were growing progressively more serious in their relationship. I knew that a confrontation could severely damage the close friendship between us, but I felt as though a lot of that had pulled apart anyway once Jake had started dating Chrystina. What did I have to lose? My illness made me feel increasingly agitated with life, and besides feeling that a confrontation was necessary, I also was in an overall mood to express anger—didn't matter who I yelled at, just as long as it was someone—and Jake was the perfect candidate. It was akin to the worst case of PMS I had ever experienced, and I felt that I was more than justified in saying something to Jake.

The afternoon they returned from vacation, Jake stopped by to check on his phone messages and take a look at his appointment schedule for the next day. Chrystina dropped him off in her police cruiser.

"I'll see you later," I heard Jake whisper before there was a soft rustling of fabric against fabric that could only mean swooping in for a kiss and then the gentle closing of the front door.

I gritted my teeth and focused down on the vegetables I was slicing. Jake walked into the kitchen.

"Hey, Grace. What's up?" He slid out a barstool and sat down.

I set down my knife and finally looked him in the eyes. "Jake, you can't do this anymore." I rubbed at my thumbnails and didn't even feel pain this time from the edges that resembled briars. I had had so much to be angry about lately that apparently I had developed calluses on my pointer fingers.

He raised an eyebrow, confused.

"Does Chrystina know yet?"

"That I'm the sexiest man alive and *People* just hasn't found me yet?" Jake swerved from side to side in the barstool and grinned like a sassy twelve-year-old. "Of course she knows *that*."

I was so tightly wound that I couldn't even laugh. "Try that your occupation is against the law."

He drummed his fingers on the countertop. "Grace, we discussed this before, remember? I'll tell her when I think it's appropriate."

"You guys have been dating for three months, Jake! What have you been telling her you're doing for a living? Mopping floors at Wal-Mart?!"

Jake glanced away. "She thinks I'm still in grad school and living on a grant from the government."

I ran my tongue across the front of my teeth and kept silent.

"I know I need to tell her, Grace," Jake's voice became a gentle plea. "But Chrystina is the best thing that's happened to me in a long time, and I don't want to lose her. I don't know how to even launch into a conversation about my job, especially since I really have kind of lied to her all along. She's going to hate me, Grace. It's going to take a lot of mental preparation for me to even *attempt* to start that kind of conversation, let alone actually go through with it. It's probably going to spell the end of our relationship."

Stupid, stupid womanizing charm. I felt my heart soften, even though he was talking about another woman. As my mind battled between continuing to berate him and easing up, I looked at him, really looked at him, and a flash on his hand caught my eye. Jake smiled sheepishly and held up his left hand, palm toward himself. I squinted in the overcast light of the morning and gasped at the thick white-gold band on his ring finger. "Are...are you—?"

He nodded. "It was kind of a whim. We still want to have a big reception for all of our friends and family to come to, but we just got caught up and eloping seemed like the right decision. It still does. I don't regret the decision at all."

"But, Jake, she doesn't even really know anything about you. And how do you even know for sure if you know the truth about her?" Finished with the knife, I threw it into the sink with a ferocity that made the utensil jump a couple of inches when it hit the stainless steel. *And whatever happened to us?!* I cried out to myself.

"Chrys and I are going to make it, Grace." He narrowed his eyes. "It's not like the relationship between you and me."

That stung, but I bit back with, "Yeah, whatever happened with that, anyway?"

"I don't know. I think you gave up on us."

"Are you kidding me?! You cheated on me the first time, and the second time I couldn't tell who you wanted—I can see clearly now it was Chrystina."

"Yeah, and I can tell that I made the right decision, because you've turned out to be an angry, self-centered b—"

Before he could even finish the word, I picked up the whole cutting board covered in vegetables and chucked it at him. He left my house with carrots clinging to his hair and cucumber juice dripping off his face. I don't know if he walked home or if Chrystina came back to give him a ride. I grabbed the box of Kleenex from the bathroom and went straight to bed.

CHAPTER TWENTY

The next couple of days Jake arrived at work as late as possible and left on the heels of his last client for the afternoon. We didn't speak to each other at all. The one time I needed to let him know something, I stole a Post-it from Keisha's desk and stuck it to his coat on the tree upstairs.

"I went on the most incredible date last night." Keisha flung her purse to the floor and herself into the swivel chair at her desk, scattering a pile of file folders. "Oh, Grace, I don't even know if I can concentrate on work today."

Oh, the drama of a nineteen-year-old's relationships. I laughed and bent to pick up the folders. "How'd you meet this guy?"

Keisha cringed and looked away from me. She plucked at some pens splayed in a rectangular plastic container in the desk corner. "You don't want to know."

I glanced up. "Keisha…"

"Can I just tell you about the date first?"

"Sure. Whatever."

"We went to that new Italian restaurant on Fourth Street. He was the perfect gentleman—opened my car door *and* the door into the restaurant, complimented me on my dress, gave me his suit jacket when I mentioned I was cold. There was a long wait for the food but it didn't even seem like it because there were zero awkward pauses in our conversation. We totally have a lot in common but not too much to make it seem like he was just agreeing with everything I said to get me to sleep with him."

Keisha continued, but I began to tune out. If she was embarrassed as to how they had met, then he probably was not as great of a guy as she tried to convince herself. The days she came back to work after break-ups were the worst—not only because she tended to take up hours of our working time with crying and low work production but also because it saddened me that she was so naïve in thinking that every next guy she met was THE ONE. All she really wanted to do was get married. Plus, I was trying to be patient and a good listener, but seriously, I had enough problems with guys that I didn't want to listen to anyone else's relationships, good or bad.

Suddenly Keisha caught my attention again. "What's up with you and Jake lately, anyway? Are you in a fight over his marriage to Chrys?"

I refrained from comment.

She must have decided that my lack of a response was a yes. "Grace, what if Chrystina really is, like, Jake's soul mate, and you're pushing her away?"

I snorted. "It's a possibility," I ground out.

"What if we plan a little get-together? Something separate from the wedding reception, whenever they're going to have that. I'll bring a date, you bring a date, and Jake and Chrystina can come. We can all get to know her better."

#

Sometimes my secretary has good ideas. So, to prove to Jake and Chrystina that I wasn't angry with them for their decision to elope or for the fact that Jake had married the "enemy," I invited David, Keisha and what's-his-name, Jake, and Chrystina over to my home for the upcoming weekend. Saturday, the day they were supposed to come over, dawned red in the morning, and the humidity was so high that I took three showers before everyone came over and still felt sweaty and as though I'd been working outside all day long. I turned on my TV an hour before everyone was set to arrive and noticed a tornado watch in the corner of the screen. A newscast was just breaking in when my doorbell rang. I switched the TV off and was surprised to see Chrystina, sans Jake, at the door.

"Hey, Grace, I thought you might need some help with the food," Chrystina said shyly. The confident attitude that she displayed when it came to her job did not carry over into real life. Jake must have told her that I hated her or something, which was definitely not true. I was merely skeptical, and I had every right to be. There were still moments when I envied her for getting to marry Jake, but I tried hard not to dwell on them. "Jake'll be over in a bit. He's mowing our lawn."

That was still so weird for me to hear her say—"our lawn." Jake's bachelor pad had never seemed as though it would be fit for a woman to live there, too, but Chrystina had managed to transform it into something kind of cute.

"That'd be great. Come in," I welcomed. I had not been planning to prepare that much food and was mostly finished putting together the few appetizers I was going to set out, but maybe I would come up with something more now since Chrystina had made such an effort to be friends.

She quietly followed me into the kitchen and leaned her back against the counter, bare, polished toes kneading the linoleum in nervous anticipation. She wrapped her arms around herself and drummed her fingers against her side. I felt guilty for making her so uncomfortable and tried to be friendlier.

"Would you like to help me make some cookies?" I asked, taking a quick look through my cupboards to see if I even owned all the ingredients for cookies, and on top of that, if any of them were past their expiration dates. I was grateful to see that I did have everything for a simple batch of chocolate chip cookies and decided that if things became too tense between us, I would just turn the mixer up to high for a long time, making it impossible for us to have a conversation.

"So, anything interesting go down at the station the past couple of days?" I asked, measuring out flour while Chrystina, eager for something practical to do with her hands, reached for the vanilla and a teaspoon.

"Well…," she looked at me out of the corner of her eye, "It's actually been really hard for me there. I moved here because I've been put in charge of a team whose top priority is to track down medical frauds. We arrested a chiropractor yesterday."

The condensation swelling on the outside of the vanilla

jar suddenly caused her grip to falter, and the organic, over-priced flavoring spat out onto the counter, the floor, the wall, and Chrystina's shirt as the dark glass fell and shattered. We both winced.

I stepped outside the bounds of the glass on the floor and pulled a dishtowel from a drawer, soaking it all up while Chrystina apologized, her face red. With a napkin, she swiped at the drips running down my wall.

With this momentary break in the conversation, I was unsure whether I should return to the previous topic, but my desire to do so won out. "So…by 'medical frauds' do you really just mean doctors who practice alternative methods? Or are you guys trying to find frauds in the normal medical field as well?"

"Some of both." Chrystina went back to measuring out ingredients. "Two of the men on my team really have it in for alternative practitioners, and so they're mostly consumed with that, but the rest of us are trying to find medical frauds in any capacity."

I nodded and tried not to let my anger get the best of me. My temper had really been flaring up a lot lately, and Chrystina didn't deserve it. Personally, I didn't understand how she could live with herself by taking part in something like that, but I did understand the desire to excel at one's job. If being a cop was what she really wanted to do, and if that involved arresting people who had committed the same "crime" her husband committed every day, then of course she would do whatever the station assigned her to do. Right? Okay, so I didn't actually think that I could do something like that, but few people I knew had the same passion for alternative treatments that I have, so I made a good effort to understand. I also decided that it was time for a subject change. "So how did you decide to become a police officer?"

Chrystina launched into a long story of her occupational history, and I found that I was actually interested—for a while I forgot about her most recent assignment. I had just pulled the first batch of cookies from the oven when Jake arrived, followed by David, and then Keisha and her man a couple of minutes later. Everyone was barely in the door when there was a loud clap of thunder and the heavy clouds burst like water balloons slapping pavement. The rain quickly transformed into large mud puddles all over my dirt driveway and some bare spots in my yard. Within minutes, large pellets of hail joined the rain, slamming into the puddles to slowly melt away their existence. We ended up all grabbing pillows off my couches and lying on the floor in the living room, watching the storm—especially the lightning— through my large picture window. I was disappointed when my weeping willow split in half, sinking and settling into the wet ground.

We played some board games, ate a little bit, and talked, and I had probably the best, least-stressed-out time I'd had in months. I even thought that I might be able to get used to the idea of Chrystina and Jake as a couple and perhaps become friends with Chrys.

# # #

The next few weeks were filled with Jake and Chrys's preparation for the celebration of their marriage. I tried to be supportive and asked occasionally about their plans, but mostly

I made myself think about unrelated subjects. It hurt too much. I wished that I could beg out of attending but knew that would only place a severe strain on the tiny amount of progress I had made on my friendship with them.

I had heard from Chrystina regarding what food would be served at the party, what flowers she was ordering, and what she would be wearing, but I had yet to find out where they were holding the event. So, one day when Chrystina was waiting around awkwardly on my main floor for Jake to finish with his "grad school work" downstairs, I set the rag aside that I had been using to wipe off my counter and asked brightly, "So, I just realized that I haven't asked where you guys decided to have your reception. Have you picked a place?"

Chrystina bit her lip and gave me a nervous smile. "Well, Jake and I were discussing it last night, and I suggested…well, Jake didn't think you would be okay with it…but I don't know, it's just so perfect, and…"

I looked at her, trying to decipher what she was telling me and wondering why I wouldn't be okay with their choice of location.

"Could we hold it in your backyard?"

I turned away and pretended to study the inside of my fridge for dinner options. How could she ask such a thing? Was she really so oblivious to Jake's and my past relationship? I was trying hard to like this woman. I genuinely was giving it my best effort. But it was becoming more and more apparent that Jake had to be lying to Chrystina constantly. She didn't know what he did for a job; she didn't know anything about the relationship between Jake and me; I assumed she didn't know what I did for a job, and I had no idea what I would tell her if she asked. That bothered me all of a sudden. Why *hadn't* she asked? I usually saw her at least two or three times a week, and she had *never asked*. Something was going on, and it made me nervous.

"Is it all right if I let you know tomorrow?" I asked, tight smile pasted politely in place.

"Of course, Grace. Thank you for considering it." She beamed, and my stomach knotted.

# # #

Hanging out with David was making me realize how selfish I was most of the time. He was constantly doing kind things for people, even people he didn't know well who expected him to help them just because they attended his church occasionally. So, in an effort to be a more loving person, I agreed to allow Jake and Chrys to hold their reception at my house. When I told them, Chrystina cheered and hugged me, and I watched Jake's expression over her shoulder. He stood a few feet away, arms crossed, and stared straight into my eyes, lips pursed. *Are you sure?* he mouthed, looking queasy.

Yes, I mouthed back. I couldn't help it. I was glad that he felt uncomfortable.

Chrystina pulled away from me and thanked me again. "Jake, let's go outside and walk around a little; we can decide where to put the tables and the food and all." She walked ahead, practically skipping with excitement, and was out my front door before Jake had even slipped both of his shoes back on.

"Grace, this might not be the best idea," he whispered,

sitting on the bench beside my door and tilting his head to lean against the wall. His eyes were closed, and he looked more and more uneasy as the seconds passed.

"Having the reception at my house?" I clarified, just in case he was referring to something else not being a good idea (like his deserting me for a hasty marriage to Chrystina, perhaps?). A small part of me still craved his attention, but I knew that, even if he were to annul his marriage, I would never go back to him. Would I?

"Yeah," he replied. "Grace, what the heck are you thinking?"

I thought through my motives a little better before answering. I had told myself that I was being unselfish by letting Chrystina have her reception at her first choice, but maybe...maybe I was actually trying to make things as weird as possible for Jake. Maybe I had known this all along and had been pushing it down, out of the way of my conscience that had gradually become more sensitive since I had started trying what David had talked about that day after the hospital. I had been spending a little bit of time reading my Bible on a few separate occasions in the past weeks, and although I hadn't gotten around to praying—it felt awkward; I didn't really know what to say—I did pick up on that I probably wasn't living my life the way I should. I never should have agreed to the reception, but it was too late to change my mind.

I shook my head and walked away.

CHAPTER TWENTY-ONE

The day of the reception was a perfect 72 degrees. I woke up with a headache and a sore jaw. I had slept an hour here, an hour there—in between the single hours of peace, I twisted and squirmed physically and emotionally. Tears soaked my pillow to the point that my face started to become red and chafed from resting against the wet fabric. A few minutes later, I would be so angry at Jake, Chrystina, and what's-her-name from forever ago that Jake left me for that I would throw the pillow onto the ground and grind my teeth together so tightly that I thought they might crack apart. Then I would pick the pillow back up again and cry some more. I even laid on my back on the carpet for a while, somehow hoping that maybe a change of location would give me a different perspective on life or at least more sleep. It didn't work. I tried to think of how I might be able to escape from the wedding reception but could come up with nothing plausible.

When my alarm sounded, I threw the covers aside and

stepped into the shower, taking a full forty-five minutes to savor the hot water. I spent forever shaving my legs, deciding to focus extra closely on removing every single hair rather than thinking about what was going to transpire in my own backyard that day and how I had made everything worse than it needed to be. I could hear people coming and going from my house, and occasionally happy voices drifted in from the yard. I had told Chrystina previously that she could use my guest bedroom to get ready in, and I had listened to hardcore, angry rock music while cleaning it up for her, screaming the lyrics at the top of my lungs. Footsteps and the rustle of clothing went from one end of my hall to the other, back and forth outside my bathroom, going to and from the guest bedroom. I stayed safely inside my large bathroom, dressing slowly, rubbing lotion across my legs and arms, and smoothing wrinkles out of my dress. I applied makeup and painted my toenails, and then spent half an hour curling my hair while the nail polish dried. I carefully selected jewelry, sprayed myself with perfume, and cursed quietly when I heard Chrystina's mom telling Chrys how beautiful she looked and how great of a guy Jake was. For a couple of minutes I thought I might throw up, but I hadn't eaten anything yet that day, and so nothing came up even though I gagged a little. There was nothing left to do—I had done everything I could to get ready, and I looked the best I had looked in a long time. I had to leave my safe haven and endure the festivities of the day.

Since Chrystina had been unable to wear a wedding dress for the actual wedding due to its spontaneity, she had purchased a wedding dress for this event. As I took a deep breath and stepped out into the hall, I nearly collided with the enormous white dress. Chrystina grabbed my arm to steady herself and grinned. "Grace, I just want to thank you again for allowing us to have the reception here. This is fantastic! I'm so happy that the weather turned out so amazing!"

Time for the fake smile. "No problem, Chrys. I'm glad the day turned out so great for you!" I gushed and gave her a hug. Perhaps this was overkill, but she didn't seem to notice.

She straightened her veil and adjusted her hair as we pulled away from each other. "Gotta keep everything perfect," she said, and I felt like it was a jab at me, but I couldn't decide for sure because her smile appeared genuine when she said it.

"Of course," I replied. "What do you need help with?" The reception was starting in half an hour; I was trying to appear to be nice, but I was actually counting on that the details were probably settled by now.

"Um…" The bride placed her hands on her hips and looked around, as if a chore for me to do was going to magically pop out of the wall. "That's really nice of you to offer, but I don't think there's anything…oh, wait!" Chrystina widened her eyes and pointed her finger at me, smiling pleadingly. "This is kind of gross, and you don't have to do it, but somebody told me a little bit ago that a lot of birds were hanging around the chairs. Will you check and make sure that the birds haven't left any messes on the chairs?"

Are you KIDDING me? This is the ONLY thing you can think of for me to help you with?! That's disgusting! I'm not doing it! "I'll take a look." As I stepped away, I dug my fingers into my thumbnails and resisted the urge to turn around and stomp on her train as she walked away, ripping the satin and leaving a gaping hole in the back of the dress. Maybe Chrys knew more than I gave her credit for. Maybe she did know I was Jake's ex and was punishing me for it. I supposed I deserved it; I had done my fair share of punishing the happy couple.

I slid into my tall strappy sandals and teetered across the grass to inspect the chairs. I didn't try very hard; I merely attempted to look as though I were doing something important. Oddly enough, the only chair in the whole place that had questionable material lingering on it was at the bridal party's table, and on the bride's chair specifically. After noticing this, I paced back and forth around that table several times, debating whether I should do the right thing and wipe the poop away or leave it and hope that she didn't notice and sat in it. David walked into my backyard at that moment, gorgeous in a tux (and real dress shoes instead of flip-flops for once!), and I knew that I had to wipe off that chair. I swiped a paper napkin from the buffet table and cleaned the chair off to the best of my ability.

"Hey, you look nice," David commented as he walked up to me.

"So do you," I said, smiling. It gave me a small measure of peace just to be near him, and I decided that if I was going to make it through the day without killing someone—or at the very least, without tripping Chrystina—I had better stick close to David.

The yard was divided up into two sections for the big event—one section contained rows of chairs for the initial ceremony (Jake and Chrys were planning to repeat their vows, since only the obligatory witnesses had been present the first time), and the other section was composed of small, white, round tables which could each seat six comfortably. Underneath a large white canopy, two long tables had been placed end-to-end and covered in white tablecloths, and silver platters with dome-shaped lids pinned the cloths in place, the food waiting to be unveiled at the proper moment. An obnoxiously large sheer silver bow decorated the back of each chair, and a thick silver candle rested in the middle of each table. Even though Chrys had told me repeatedly the details of the meal, I still had no idea what we were going to eat. I was becoming quite skilled at tuning her out and nodding at the appropriate times.

The wedding party fluttered around on my deck, two of the groomsmen smoking and one of the bridesmaids flirting and laughing with the best man. The rest of them leaned against the railing, looking down on the guests milling around below. A dark blue uniform caught my eye, and I turned to see a policeman who must have been one of Chrystina's co-workers strolling casually around my yard, studying my flowers, picking a fallen leaf off from a table, and inspecting the guests a little too closely. I turned away from him, refusing to worry on this already stressful day, and opened my mouth to speak to David when I noticed that another cop was walking along the other side of my yard, talking on his cell phone. It was inevitable that Chrystina's co-workers would attend the reception, but I was getting nervous. At least everything was outside, and even if one of them went inside to use the bathroom, there shouldn't be anything upstairs that would give away my illegal activity.

The deejay began playing "Canon in D" and the guests congregated in the chairs, their conversations dying out as Jake slid into his spot up front. David and I took seats toward the back, and Candace slipped in on the other side of me at the last minute. She gave me a side hug and whispered, "Are you doing okay?"

I shrugged.

She smiled sympathetically. "Let me know if there's anything I can do to make the situation better," she said quietly.

I nodded my thanks. David glanced at me in concern. "Is something wrong?" he whispered.

I could hear huffs from the guests behind us, angry that we were being disruptive to the service. The bridesmaids and groomsmen were beginning to file in. "I'm fine," I told David.

My heart nearly stopped when I took my first good look at Jake. I couldn't decide who looked better in a tux—David or Jake. Jake, outgoing as he was, actually looked nervous standing up front, and once again I felt slightly guilty that I had contributed to the awkwardness of the situation. The bridal march began, and I reluctantly turned to watch Chrystina. I heard her mom gasp as Chrys walked in and several whispers of "Look how beautiful she is." As she advanced to the front, approaching the empty spot beside Jake, I couldn't help but think, *It should be me up there.*

During the twenty-minute ceremony, I ran through song lyrics in my head, trying so hard to think of anything other than the people in front of me. I mentally said the alphabet backwards twice, counted by sevens up to 497, and tried to remember poems that I had learned in elementary school. I must have had a really bizarre expression on my face while trying to think of the words to "Wynken, Blynken, and Nod," because Candace gripped my arm and whispered, "Are you sure you're okay? You look like you're going to cry or pass out or something."

I jerked out of my reverie to notice that Jake and Chrystina were walking down the aisle, happily arm-in-arm. What a bad spot to tune in on. At least I had somehow missed the "You may kiss the bride" part.

"Yeah, I was just distracting myself," I muttered back. "I'm going to go in my house for a bit and skip the receiving line."

David overheard this and offered quietly to go inside with me. I sort of wanted to be alone but decided it might keep me calmer to have him with me, so I agreed to his offer. As we entered the house, I went straight downstairs to my office, and David followed. I collapsed into Keisha's swivel chair, and he lingered at the corner of the desk, clearly unsure as to what he should do to help. I had never explained to him about Jake before, and I wasn't sure if it would be weird for me to talk about it.

"Is something going on that I might be able to help with?" David asked hopefully.

"Um…" I straightened up a pile of papers on Keisha's desk and played with a pen, removing the cap and sliding it back on again, over and over. "I'll just give you the short version of it. At one point, Jake and I were engaged, and then he left me for someone else. Over the past few months, we'd grown kind of close again, and then he found Chrystina. Today is just kind of a weird day for me."

I halfway expected David to be angry about it. I mean, he and I weren't officially dating, but we had been hanging out more together (and the AIDS secret had kind of bonded us), and I knew it was taboo to talk about past relationships with your current significant other. But this was me, mistakes and all, and it was probably best to get everything out in the open.

"And now they're holding their wedding reception at your house?" David asked, incredulous. "I think you're bearing this remarkably well."

I snorted. "You can't see how much of a mess I am inside. I can't *wait* for this day to be over."

The phone on the desk rang, and I picked it up automatically. "HP Health Services."

"Grace?" It was my mother.

"Hi, Mom." It was random for her to call right now; I thought for sure I had told her about the reception scheduled for today, and she should know that I would be busy (although obviously I was not).

"Grace, Grandpa Hampton is in the hospital on a ventilator. He might not make it through the night."

I gasped. How had he become so ill so quickly, and I hadn't even been over to visit yet? I thought through the past few weeks and realized, with a sad sigh, that it had, in reality, been months since he had been diagnosed. My parents had been trying to get me to come home for weeks and weeks now, and I had let time slip away, caught up in my own problems, and now I might not even get to have one last conversation with my grandpa. I started to cry for the thousandth time in twenty-four hours, and David looked at me in alarm.

Suddenly, the most brilliant thought ever occurred to me, and I stated, "Mom, I'll be there as soon as I can. I'm leaving right now." I really wanted to see my grandpa, and this was about the only acceptable situation that could get me out of staying through the reception.

"Okay. We'll see you in a little while, Grace."

I hung up the phone and rose out of the chair. "I have to go home," I stated to David. "My grandpa is dying."

"Oh, Grace," he said sadly and reached over to hug me. It was the closest I had ever been to David—he was much less touchy than Jake had ever been—and I relished his strong arms and the scent of his cologne. I clung to him, resting my head on his shoulder, and cried just a little bit more before backing away and swiping at my eyes and nose with a Kleenex.

"I guess I'll just go tell Jake and Chrystina what's going on and then I'll take off," I said. "It sounds like he's really bad; I don't even know if I'll make it in time."

"I'll drive you," David offered abruptly. "You really shouldn't drive yourself in this condition."

I started to protest. We weren't officially a couple; it definitely was not his duty to spend the day with me and my grieving family, whom he had never met previous to this somber occasion.

"Grace, I don't even have to preach tomorrow; a missionary is coming in to do the service," he interrupted. "There's nothing else I'm supposed to be doing right now except helping you out. I *want* to help you."

Well, when he put it that way…"Okay," I conceded.

CHAPTER TWENTY-TWO

It took only a few minutes to let Jake and Chrystina know what was going on. I was surprised to see some genuine sympathy in Jake's eyes. Although he had never met my grandpa before, he had met my parents and a few other members of my family, and I guess he must have still felt a bit of a connection to us. I spoke with Candace after my brief conversation with the happy couple, and before I had told her that David was coming with me, she offered to drive me.

I cleared my throat. "Thank you, but actually, David said he would take me," I said quietly.

Candace looked pleasantly surprised, and I saw a smile competing with the serious, intense expression on her face. "Oh, okay," she exclaimed. "Even better." She smiled slyly. "Oh, and don't worry about anything here—I'll make sure everything gets cleaned up. Call me if you think of anything else you need me to do for you on this end."

I hugged and thanked her again, and, after one more

quick look around at the reception and once again being grateful that I was able to flee the scene, I headed toward my house to grab a few things and take off.

David had left briefly to fill his car with gas, and I changed out of my dress and into jeans, pulling my curls into a ponytail before packing some random things into an overnight bag. I had no idea if I would be staying there, or if I'd be coming back tonight, or what would happen, since David was driving me. I wasn't sure what he was planning to do.

A few people were moving around in the kitchen, grabbing more food from my fridge and discussing the pros and cons of outdoor weddings. High heels clicked across the linoleum in the kitchen and the bathroom, and I cringed at how much cleaning I was going to have to do after these people left. The ground was a little damp outside from some rain a couple of days ago, and I knew that there had to be dirt getting tracked across my cream-colored carpet. I refused to let myself get worked up again over my poor decision to hold the reception here; I needed to concentrate on my grandpa and his condition right now. When I walked out of my bedroom, bag in hand, I passed a police officer on his way to the bathroom. He glanced at me curiously but didn't say anything as I blew past him.

As I gathered a couple of bottled waters from my refrigerator, David walked in, dressed in jeans as well. Even though I wanted him to be comfortable on the long ride to the hospital, I was slightly disappointed that he was no longer wearing the tux. As I studied him longer, though, I decided that maybe he looked even better in casual wear than in something formal. *Grace, there are so many more important things to think about.*

"Would you like me to take your bag?" he asked, reaching out for the heavy duffel slung over my shoulder (in no state of mind to make trivial decisions, I had ended up flinging whatever random pieces of clothing I found first into my bag. I didn't even know if I had a matching outfit in there).

I gladly handed it over, hiked my purse up higher onto my shoulder, and followed David out to his car, where he hefted my bag in beside his in the backseat. I guess that answered my question—he was prepared to hang out with me for a couple of days if necessary. I breathed a sigh of relief; it was comforting to know that someone was looking out for me.

As we drove away, I looked back at my house and caught a glimpse of Jake tilting his head back and laughing, champagne sloshing in his hand. Chrystina, more gorgeous than I could ever hope to be in her size two designer dress, touched his arm lightly and stood on her toes, reaching up for a kiss. I bit my lip and swore that I would never let that man hurt me ever again.

Beside me, David hummed some song I vaguely remembered hearing at church and turned the air conditioning colder.

I was startled awake by my cell phone vibrating in my jacket pocket. Candace.

"Hey."

"Hey, Grace, I don't want to give you anything else to worry about, but I just thought I should make you aware of something…"

I sat up; I had fallen asleep hunched over awkwardly against the window. "What?"

"Well, you know how all of Chrystina's cop friends were hanging out here for the reception? At one point I walked into

the house and saw one of them coming up from downstairs.
When I asked him if I could help him with something, he just
said that he was looking for the bathroom. I pointed it out,
but—Grace, you know we put up signs pointing the way from
the front door to the bathroom. Anyone who can read and follow arrows should not have had a problem finding the bathroom. Had you picked things up downstairs, or was a bunch of
your medical stuff still sitting out?"

"I hadn't counted on anyone going downstairs. I have no
idea what was out down there." I racked my brain for a mental
picture of what my office had looked like when I had been down
there with David earlier in the day, but I had been so distressed
that I hadn't paid much attention to my surroundings. It wasn't
my habit to leave bottles of pills and homeopathics lying around,
but I had been so scattered the past few days with the reception
coming up that half the time I didn't know what I was doing.
Once I had caught myself throwing away patient files when I
was supposed to be sorting through bills.

"Well, I just thought I should let you know…Grace, it
was weird. I just felt like I should warn you."

"I appreciate it," I said, taking a sip of water. "But I can't
worry about that right now. I'll deal with it whenever I get back
home."

"Okay. I'll talk to you later, Grace."

"Bye, Candace. Thank you."

My mom met us in the waiting room at the hospital. She
didn't even realize that David was with me at first, just gave me a
hug and led me away to my grandpa's room, arm draped around
my shoulder. David trailed behind, allowing us some space.

Once we walked in the room crowded with close to twenty of my relatives, though, it was impossible not to notice that he was stalking us. My mother shot him a careful smile and looked at me questioningly.

I shrugged my shoulders, smiled, and nearly laughed when I saw my twenty-year-old cousin Shelly checking David out. She gave me a grin of approval and two thumbs up.

The next few days passed in a blur. My grandpa never did wake up enough to talk to me, but it was still comforting to be near him as he lay dying and to be surrounded by my family. I couldn't imagine how difficult this must be for my aunt and uncle who were also suffering from the same illness—they both had to be wondering whether this would be a picture of them in a couple of months. David came and went, staying with me for half a day or a full day at a time, and then driving back to help out one of the parishioners at his church or work on next week's sermon for a little while. On Saturday, as David drove me back home after the funeral, I sat silently in his car the whole way, reflecting on death and my job and what I should perhaps do differently with my life, but I didn't say anything to him about it, because I figured that whatever he had to say might not be what I wanted to hear at the moment. When we arrived at my house, he reached across the seat and grasped my hand. "Is there anything else I can do for you, Grace?"

"Not right now," I replied quietly. "I really appreciate all of your help the last week, though. You've been amazingly supportive, and that has helped more than you could know."

I leaned over and hugged him awkwardly across the seat, and then I slid out, and he helped me carry my luggage inside.

The house was empty since I had been forced to cancel all of my appointments for the week, and Jake was still on his honeymoon. David and I said goodbye, and then I ate some couscous and went to sleep.

# # #

That week, strange, sad vacation that it was, was truly a blessing, because later that night, long after my lights were out and I was lying in bed, still awake and smiling at the thought that mine and David's relationship was going so well, my cell phone rang. I didn't recognize the number but answered anyway.

It was Chrystina. She must have gotten my number from Jake. "Grace? Grace! I need you to listen to me. Someone turned you in. You've got to get out of town. The police are coming to your house tomorrow to arrest you."

"What?!" I sat up in bed, heart pounding.

"Grace, I found out," she said quietly.

I clenched the sheets so tightly I thought the blood might explode out of my hand. "Found out what?" I asked in a growl.

"About yours and Jake's business. My team had heard some things, and they...they...found some evidence of it at your house during the wedding reception." She actually sounded afraid. *I* was the one about to go to jail, and *Chrystina* was afraid.

"Why are you giving me a warning at all? Are you outside my house with your team right now?" My heart thudded wildly, and I rose out of bed, pulling sweatpants on over my sleep shorts and a sweatshirt on over my cami. I swept the hair out of my face and lifted the corner of my blinds, peering at my driveway. I didn't see any headlights, but they could be out there, using Chrystina to lure me outside, making me think I had time to get away, when really they were just impatient and didn't want to wait any longer to arrest me, didn't want to give me time to cause any more *damage* to the *population*. I could feel a scream building up inside, and it served Chrystina right if I screamed into her ear and burst her eardrum, causing her permanent hearing loss. Oooooh, I could just strangle…

"*NO*, Grace, I want to give you time to get away; I—I don't know how I feel about yours and Jake's business, but until I've decided, I just need you to hide."

"Well, what is Jake doing? Would you really turn your own husband in?"

"No, of course not; he's on his way out, too." She sounded slightly unsure even as she made that comment.

I wondered whether to respond to the doubt in her voice but decided I was far too angry to talk any longer. I hung up.

I closed my phone and shoved clothes into a suitcase. I would go to Candace's house; I wasn't sure who else to go to. My parents would panic more than necessary if I went to their house, but Candace understood as well as I did that risk came with the bioenergetics territory. I swept the remaining bottles from my cabinet into my suitcase, crammed patient files into a second suitcase, and tucked my laptop and accompanying hand cradle into a tote bag. All of the strange books I had lying around were probably incriminating enough, but there was no way I could pack them all up and take them with me, so I grabbed the ones that had been the most fascinating to me recently—two about AIDS and another about pancreatic cancer—and left the rest behind. I darted through Jake's office as well, confiscating his patient files and some all-natural pain pills sitting on his desk. I briefly tore through desk drawers in both of our offices, pulling random things out and sticking them in a third suitcase. Finally, I called Keisha and warned her not to show up at my house the next day for work.

Through the haze of hurriedness, I suddenly thought I heard the tornado siren. No time to consider things now. I needed to get out while I could. I was still suspicious that the police might be sitting in my driveway, laughing that I thought I had a chance to get away.

I roared down my driveway and into the road with barely a glance backward to see if there was a car coming. This storm was far worse than the one the night of the party. Rain pounded the windshield with the force of falling boulders, and I was speeding so fast that when I took my left hand off the steering wheel to twist on my wipers I nearly drove into the ditch. The puddles collecting on the road winked in the moonlight and streetlamps, playing tricks on my mind by making me think teens were running across the road, playing chicken. I momentarily slammed on the brakes to prevent impact before realizing no one else was out tonight. No one else was stupid enough to drive around while the tornado siren was sounding. The wind swept a fallen power line, sparking with electric venom, into my path. I swerved into the oncoming lane, rolled over two opossums frozen with fear on the asphalt (*thump, thump*), and darted back into my own lane. Tiny green leaves like fresh peas were scattered all over the ground, and sticks ranging in size from pencils to flagpoles dotted the ditch and the street. I turned onto

a familiar side road, one composed of gravel and, now, minia-
ture bogs. I could hardly think straight. Normally I freaked out
in bad weather, but tonight my fear of arrest consumed the few
thoughts that actually connected in my brain. Colliding with a
tornado seemed like a vacation compared to a prison sentence.

Two hours later, when I pulled into Candace's driveway,
I realized that I hadn't called her to tell her I was coming. My
hands were shaking, bound to the steering wheel like ropes. It
took me a full three minutes to pry them off. The storm had
cleared; the first rays of dawn were streaming into my weary
eyes. I nearly fell out of my car, my legs too tense to function
properly. I dragged two of my bags from the trunk and went up
to her front door.

# # #

Candace graciously took me into her small home and let
me stay on her couch. I spilled everything to her, including my
fear that I had pancreatic cancer, and she immediately offered to
solve that problem for me right then and there. She powered up
her computer, and I obediently let her test me.

I decided that maybe God really did care about me after
all. There was no trace of any cancer in my body. I had a collection of viruses, which were probably what had been making me
ill so frequently, but no cancer. Candace gave me some homeopathic remedies to begin taking and then I went to bed while she
continued getting ready for her day.

When I woke up mid-afternoon, I decided to call my
answering machine at home and check for messages. There was

a cheerful one from Anna, letting me know that she was doing better and wanted to set up her next appointment, but the next message was from a voice that I didn't recognize at first. I had to listen to it three times before I could understand who it was. The woman sounded awful, but I was able to pick out that it was Lauryn.

"Grace Hampton, I heard about you from Anna. She claims you might be able to *help* me. I can't believe you're giving that poor, sweet girl false hope! You're stealing her family's money right out from under them, and she's going to die, probably quicker than if she'd chosen chemo. I *know* you're the same Grace I met at church and who came to the hospital with David that one day. I want you to know that I'm going to report you to the police. Con artists like you need to be put in jail."

I gasped. What had Anna told her? Anna had told *me* that she was feeling better. Lauryn, with her "the world is out to get me" attitude, must have twisted Anna's joyful words around to fit her own idea of alternative treatments.

Well, no one knew that I was at Candace's. I supposed I would have to leave her house soon and figure out somewhere else to go. I had known that this would probably happen someday, but I had hoped that it was years, perhaps decades, away.

I decided to walk down to the end of Candace's driveway to get her mail and clear my head a little. As I approached the street, the sound of speeding cars and sirens caught my attention. My heart galloped, and I quickly assured myself that they weren't here for me. There had to be an emergency farther down the road. I opened the mailbox, pulled out a magazine and two bills, and started walking back toward the house.

I was only halfway up the driveway when the whole entourage pulled in behind me. I turned around, a guilty look most definitely prominent on my face.

A policeman burst out of the driver's side of the car closest to me, gun pointed straight at me. "Stop right there!"

I had already stopped, so I dropped the mail to the ground and lifted my hands in the air.

"Is that her?" I heard the policeman say to someone in the car.

Chrystina rose out of the front passenger seat, and Jake slid out of the back.

"That's her," Jake said, and Chrystina nodded.

The first policeman approached me with handcuffs. "Grace Hampton, you are under arrest for the possession and distribution of illegal medicine."

I stared at Jake, devastated tears clouding my vision. The policeman roughly slapped the cuffs onto my wrists, and I felt the metal scrape across my skin. He tugged me toward the car. "Jake, I don't understand…" I whimpered. I hated to sound so wimpy, but I was truly confused. If they were arresting me and were also aware of Jake's participation in my business (as Chrystina had shared on the phone earlier), then why was he un-cuffed and acting free as a bird? I mean, as angry as I was at Jake for all of the trouble he had caused me, I didn't honestly want him to go to jail, but seriously, what was going on?

Jake looked away from my probing gaze, focusing instead on Chrystina. Chrystina looked slightly regretful but also refused to look into my eyes, talking softly to one of her fellow officers instead.

I thought of Candace inside. Were they about to haul her off to jail, too? I was upset with myself for fleeing to her house and endangering her. I should have gone to a hotel.

The officer who had been driving the vehicle carrying Jake and Chrys switched over to one of the other police cars, handing his keys to Chrystina. They had nestled me into the backseat; Jake had moved into the passenger seat. All of the vehicles pulled out; no one arrested Candace, and I briefly pondered whether Candace had realized yet that I was missing.

There was an extremely awkward silence for a full two minutes while Chrystina followed the parade of police.

I gathered my emotions and cleared my throat. "Someone needs to explain. Now. Jake, I don't want to be rude, but why, exactly, aren't you back here with me?!"

He turned slowly to face me. "I'm sorry, Grace. I had to do it."

"What—what are you talking about?" Had he honestly played a role in turning me in?

Chrystina produced a heartless laugh. "Oh, come on, Grace, you know you would do the same thing if it meant saving your own skin. Don't worry; I'll make sure you get the lightest sentence possible."

"Jake, you ratted me out?" I whispered, tears welling up. "You actually made a deal with them to keep yourself out of jail?"

He wasn't facing me anymore, but through the haze of pain swelling in my tear ducts, I thought I saw him bite his lower lip. The car, now on the expressway, sped ever closer to my incarcerated future.

"Are you going to turn Candace in, too?" I asked.

There was a barely noticeable shake of his head.

No, he wasn't going to.

I caught Chrystina's gaze in the rearview mirror. We had pulled off the expressway and were stopped at the end of the off-ramp, stuck behind three other police cars all waiting to make the right turn to the station. She had absolutely nothing that she could pretend to be distracted by, and so I knew now was the best time to ask. Jake certainly wasn't willing to give me too many answers.

"Chrys? What kind of a deal did you guys make?"

She watched me in the rearview mirror and a tiny bit of remorse appeared in her eyes. "Grace, I have to do my job. If I protected criminals, I would be in a crazy amount of trouble. I've been a part of this medical fraud team for months now, and I've learned what to look for. I've suspected you were up to something for a while, especially since the break-in, and the way Jake seemed to avoid the topic of his career was definitely odd. A couple of tips have been called in to the station in the past month, and then the day of the wedding reception one of the other officers saw some suspicious materials on your desk downstairs. We've been investigating while you were with your family. I tried to protect Jake from it all," she glanced over at him and smiled, "but the others on my team found out that he was involved in your business as well. He agreed to, um…" her hands suddenly gripped the steering wheel tighter as her gaze darted out the window. "He agreed to testify against you and give up his medical practice permanently in exchange for freedom and a small fine."

My mouth fell open. I stared at Jake. He was bent over, his shoulders shaking as he cried silently. He had betrayed me before; I don't know why I was surprised that it had happened again. Somehow, though, I was too shocked to cry or even to be angry. I couldn't turn my eyes away from Jake the entire rest of the ride. Even as I was directed out of the vehicle, I kept my eyes locked on him. Chrystina escorted me inside and into a cell, where I sank onto the bunk and continued to picture Jake's devastated expression, a photograph of him chained in my mind. As I closed my eyes to the bare walls and poor lighting, more memories of Jake mixed in together, swirling in a black and white vortex through my head. Depressed Jake sitting in the cop car; Jake the "dirty bum" eating Candace's tortilla chips; Jake chasing the boys who stole his paycheck; depressed Jake sitting in the cop car; Jake proposing to me; Jake holding up his wedding band; Jake sleeping on my couch to protect me; depressed Jake sitting in the cop car; Jake laughing before kissing Chrystina…on and on and on.

The door to the cell swung open. "Grace Hampton? We're ready for you in the interrogation room now."

CPSIA information can be obtained at www.ICGtesting.com
Printed in the USA
BVOW030817060912

299474BV00001BA/3/P